Next to You
Honeybrook Hollow

Nora Everly

To Lori, for the inspiration.

&

To Elizabeth, thank you.

&

To anyone who has ever been frozen in the snow or
otherwise.
Open your heart, your life is waiting.

Chapter 1
Lucy

I never should have left my house. More importantly, I should have deleted all the dating apps from my phone, like I'd promised myself. But sadly, there was still a little glimmer of hope in my heart, and I had stupidly agreed to meet my latest attempt at a happily ever after at my favorite taco place for dinner.

I should have known better. Past experiences should have predicted how this evening would go. We'd meet, exchange pleasantries, tuck into some food, maybe have a drink. But then I'd find out he was only out for a bit of "fun," or he was living in his mother's basement and looking for a new mommy to take care of him. I'd also had enough of men who already had a wife; I mean, really? Bad tippers, bad manners, bad hygiene, bad, bad, bad. I need to stick to my man ban. Being alone was better.

The date had lasted ten minutes. He informed me women should always wear dresses and heels on a first date. Then he said my butt was too big for the jeans I had on. He didn't like it when women wore dark lipstick and joked that I should have made more of an effort to impress him. So, I wasted what remained of my delicious margarita on his face, ordered takeout tacos, and got the hell out of there. Men were good for nothing but trouble, and I was done with all of them.

That last glimmer of hope was dead now, killed by yet another terrible date.

RIP, hope. It was nice knowing you.

Seriously, all I had wanted was to line up a second date, which, in retrospect, was a bad idea. New Year's Eve was coming up, and I wanted a midnight kiss. It was getting close, and I'd never had one. Something about starting the new year with a kiss—with hope—felt like the change I needed.

So much for that.

My only consolation was the bag of tacos I had bought to comfort myself when I got home. I should be putting my feet up on the coffee table, binge-watching something mindless, wearing my pajamas, and enjoying my freedom to do whatever the hell I wanted right now.

Instead, I was half-buried in a leftover snowbank, huddled inside my car with nothing but a sad bag full of tacos and a whole lot of regret to keep me company.

Thank goodness I was able to spin into this colossal pile of leftover fluffy white bull crap after I lost control on that patch of ice a half mile back, or I'd probably have hit the median or a freaking tree. I could be dead or unconscious right now.

Sadly, both those things might be preferable to this illogical panic that had settled into my soul over the last ten minutes. I was freaking out, and I would never live this down, not ever.

I was a local, for elf's sake—born and raised in Honeybrook Hollow, Oregon, one of the little villages that dotted the side of the highway on the way up to Mt. Hood. Now, I was just another dumbass stuck in a ditch, no better than an out-of-towner on a ski trip. But worse than being stuck, I panicked as if I hadn't had a grand old time hiking through this stupid forest for fun. Granted, I rarely hiked at night or in the winter. Maybe I should cut myself a break. And maybe I should never take a back road ever again. I'd stick to the highway from now on.

I took another peek outside.

Could darkness loom?

More specifically, could it hover with menacing intent outside a car window?

Stop it, Lucy.

But I'm stuck out here, and my cell phone has no signal, and it's dark as pitch, and I'm pissed off and scared, damn it.

I touched my cell phone screen, craving the little bit of light it provided. Unfortunately, there was still no signal, so I could not call for help. Of all the nights to be without service, it had to be this one.

The snow had lightly fallen for hours. When I left, it was the pretty, fluffy kind that sparkled but didn't stick. I ignored the steady increase as I drove down the mountain.

Damn it, I couldn't even sit here and eat the freaking tacos because fear had twisted my gut into a pathetic knot, and I'd lost my appetite. I glanced at the bag with a derisive snort.

I had to quit freaking out. It was useless.

Forget your feelings.

Think of the tacos.

Think of going home and getting into a piping hot bubble bath with the tacos. You don't need some dumbass man in your life.

With a sudden surge of bravery, I grabbed my emergency snow shovel from the floorboard and got out to dig out the rear end. I could turn on my flashers and hopefully be seen by a passerby. The flashers weren't doing me any good buried beneath the snow, and I didn't want to turn the car back on until the exhaust was cleared.

I created enough space to restart the vehicle safely, but there was no way I could dig myself out completely. The front end was completely buried and likely damaged.

Headlights in the distance gave me hope but it quickly faded as the car sped past. I shook my head in dismay. First, they were going way too fast for the road conditions, and second, *what the heck?* How had they not noticed my flashers? *Or me?*

The following cars drove right by as if I wasn't even there. And anyone driving this late on this road had to be a local. They were lucky it was too dark for me to recognize their cars, because—*rude.*

I considered walking home. But walking alone alongside a dark and frigid mountain road was never a good idea. Heck, standing out here was probably stupid. I mean, I'd seen enough horror movies throughout my life to know absolutely everything about my current situation was precarious.

My grandma once told me I could light up a room, and we all know what happens to people who could do that.

I was in prime serial killer hunting grounds right now. My cousin Remy was a forest ranger. Get a few beers into him down at Twilight Trails Tavern, and he'd start spitting all kinds of forest facts that no one wanted to hear about.

Do you know how many bodies are found here each year? I shuddered at the thought. The Mt. Hood National Forest was pretty much a graveyard for hikers with no sense of direction, people who a rabid animal had attacked—seriously, watch out for squirrels, they aren't your friends—and victims of who knew what kind of crimes. They'd also found abandoned cars out here too—like mine. I was so screwed.

My heart rate skyrocketed as I contemplated how much trouble I was in. It was so freaking cold, and I was not dressed to be outside like this—my mother's lectures about proper winter attire echoed in my head as I rubbed my cold hands over my upper arms and tried to stop my teeth from chattering. I blew into my hands and looked helplessly up the road.

I was not about to become some frostbitten dead body to be discovered by Ranger Remy and his buds on one of their hikes, then told as a drunken warning story in a bar. No way, not this girl.

I climbed back into the driver's seat and locked the door to wait for help. Snow was melting in my hair; the icy drip of it went down the back of my hoodie, and I shivered. All I had to warm myself with was a ratty old blanket in the back seat. With a reach, I grabbed it and wrapped myself up. The twin olfactory delights of motor oil and dirty tire odor assaulted me as I inhaled a deep breath to calm my ricocheting heartbeat.

I looked up as sloppy, wet snowflakes plopped on my windshield.

A light dusting of snow, my ass.

This was not supposed to be happening right now. The weather report was wrong. I trusted you, Skipper McFadden! If I survived, I would send a strongly worded letter to him and his team of so-called meteorologists. I swear I could see ice forming on the road.

Hopefully, someone I knew would stop, and I could convince them to keep my tragic little dating foray out of the town gossip circles—the Honeybrook Hollow busybodies would have a field day with this. I also said a silent prayer that I didn't lose the rest of my mind while I waited for help or for my cell signal to come back. The power must be out. Or a cell phone tower or whatever. Frustration got the better of me, and I slammed my hand on the center console.

The last thing I needed was for word of this to get out. My mother was already overprotective. I mean, I was thirty-three years old, a fully grown woman, and she still gave me crap if I didn't text her every evening to say goodnight and let her know I was still alive. The thought of me stranded on the side of the road all night in the dark might give her a heart attack.

Hopefully someone from Cassidy's Automotive

would happen to drive by in one of their tow trucks, and I could give them an extra big tip in exchange for their silence. They were known to cruise these roads in their huge trucks all winter. Each year, they made a killing by pulling people out of snowbanks and ditches and towing them to safety. They served the entire area from Sweetbriar to Honeybrook Hollow and all the way up the mountain to the Timberline Lodge.

Just as long as it wasn't Spencer.

Spencer Cassidy and I were in the same grade all through school, except for first grade, and I'd had a tiny, little, hopeless crush on him since forever. I had to be losing it if I was thinking of him right now.

He was that old high school crush that never went away but had gotten worse as an adult, probably because the fantasy I'd built up of him in my mind was so much better than my reality. Add to that, he'd only seemed to get more handsome as the years went on—taller, broader, more muscular. And his blue eyes? Irresistible. We rarely spoke beyond a "Hey, how are you?" But after each interaction, I always ended up kicking myself for not letting him know I was into him.

Well, at least if I were close to death, my last memory would be a happy one. Ahh, Spencer Cassidy, you have no idea how much you have unwittingly impacted my life.

I heaved out a huge sigh and rechecked my phone. No bars. No help. No hope.

Except...

I spun in my seat as headlights in the distance behind me lit up my car. I slowly turned to watch as they passed, slowed down, and backed up to stop in front of my vehicle. I stared into the glare—dare I get my hopes up?

I squinted into the light. It was a red tow truck, and the Cassidy's Automotive logo was emblazoned in bright white script across the rear. My salvation was near. I could feel it in my partially frozen bones.

YES!

All the Cassidy trucks were painted fire engine red, and there was no mistaking them around here.

It looked like I wouldn't freeze to death tonight, after all. I let out a massive sigh of relief and counted to ten as I attempted to gather my thoughts and contain my almost panic attack.

I watched as a man, tall and broad, got out. As he headed my way, I decided I didn't even care if it was Spencer. All I wanted was to go home, run as hot a bath as I could stand, and finally eat these damn tacos. Cold or not, it would be the best snack of my life.

The *tap, tap, tap* on the window sent a surge of anticipatory awareness through my body as I watched, squinting into the glare of the taillights as he got closer and closer until—

Of course.

It was Spencer and not one of his brothers or even his father.

Okay, I admit it. I lied.

I did care that it was him *so much*.

Way too much when I thought of how many years had passed since we were back at Sweetbriar High together. I had sat next to or behind him in every class because his last name was Cassidy, and mine was Darlington, and most of our teachers had put us in alphabetical order. I was pretty sure the back of his head would be embedded in my mind for all eternity.

Sometimes, he would go a few weeks too long between haircuts, and his hair would get wavy. The way it curled over his collar was magical; it looked so soft. The great tragedy of my life was that I'd never be able to run my fingers through it.

I heaved out a sigh.

At this point, pining from afar was second nature to me. When it came to dating, friendships, love, and relationships, I always went in with an open mind and heart, hoping to find someone who would really see me, someone who would appreciate who I was and who might grow to love me. Yet each time, I came away losing another slice of my confidence and heart and retreated further into myself.

Maybe that's why dating wasn't fun anymore. I needed to find my spark. With each failed try, my desire to let myself be vulnerable had faded further away.

I heaved another dramatic sigh and lowered my window as he approached.

"Hey, Spencer," I mumbled without looking up at him.

"Lucy? Is that you?" He hunkered down with bent knees, leaning his arms on my open window. Snowflakes clung to his hair as he smiled at me softly, with his eyes filled with concern. "I thought I recognized your car. I haven't seen you around town in a while. What are you doing out this late? Are you okay?"

He recognized my car? How on earth would he know what kind of car I drove? And how would he know I haven't been in town lately? I was on deadline, writing my latest Larry the Llama children's book until last week, meaning I'd been living off coffee and takeout. The light of day was something I had not seen in months.

I wrinkled my nose in confusion, struggling to find something to say to him.

A shiver shot through me at the very idea of being

recognized by him, of being *seen*. But I shut it down before my juvenile imagination could run even wilder than it already was. How very high school of me.

"Indeed it is I, Lucy Darlington, the first. Much to my shame." I rolled my lips between my teeth, hoping to stem the flow of nonsense words that decided to pop out of nowhere in a crisp, British accent. My cheeks heated enough to thaw the snowbank surrounding my poor car. *Why am I like this?*

His gorgeous blue eyes lit up in amusement. "Nothing to be ashamed of. Getting stuck in the snow up here happens to all of us at some point. It's inevitable, like a rite of passage. No one was expecting this much snow. It wasn't in the forecast."

"Right, I totally didn't expect this." I waved a hand around for emphasis. "I never would have left the house. Freaking Skipper McFadden."

"Oh yeah, he's clueless. Hey, is that Taco Time? I'm starving. I'll trade you a taco for a tow."

"I would be happy to share my tacos. But I seriously doubt something like this has ever happened to you. There is no way you've been stuck up here."

He shrugged as a grin tipped up the corner of his luscious mouth. "Only because I'm usually driving one of these tow trucks. Come on, let me help you. No charge for old friends."

Old friends. I'd take it.

I grabbed my purse and the tacos and opened the door, shuddering from the sudden sharp blast of cold and the warm grip of his hand as I slid mine into his. What a gentleman. A tall, dark, and hot, ripped to shreds, sexy gentleman. I'd seen him jogging around Honeybrook Hollow from time to time. I knew about all those muscles he was hiding under his winter jacket, thank you very much.

He led me to the truck, which was pulled as far to the side as he could. "It's quite a way up. Let me help you."

"Thanks." He opened the driver's door for me, holding me by my elbow as I put a foot on the running board.

"Steady now." His hand tightened, sliding to my upper arm as he took the taco bag from my other hand.

"How do you manage to get up here all the time?" I asked as I struggled to hoist my leg far enough to climb. My jeans were too tight, dang it. They were wet and sticking to me too.

He let out a chuckle. "I'm six foot five. What are you? About five four?"

"Something like that," I murmured as I clambered into the cab and over the console to settle into the passenger seat.

I was five three without shoes and reaching things

on high shelves without some type of assistance was not one of my strengths.

"Here ya go." He passed me the bag and my purse with a wink. "Save one for me."

Trying my best to ignore the wink, I answered. "I'll let you have them all if you can get me home. Thank you, Spencer. I really appreciate this. I had no idea what I was going to do. Panic was about to set in. I was this close."

He chuckled as I held my thumb and pointer a half inch apart for reference.

"I'm glad I happened by. It's late, and the thought of you being out here alone is, um—yeah. I don't much like that thought. Anything could happen on this road." He let out a breath before continuing. "Tacos are awesome, but getting stuck in a snowbank is not. I'm not trying to lecture you. Just keep that in mind for next time."

"I've already learned my lesson. There will be no more after-dark excursions to Taco Time. At least not in winter, believe me. And hey, can we keep this between the two of us?"

I didn't mention my unfortunate date. No one needed to know about that.

"Absolutely. These lips are sealed." He mimed turning a key in a lock over his grinning lips. "I won't say a word. Your secrets are safe with me."

"Thanks." I breathed, stupidly thrilled at the notion of sharing a secret with him. Even one as innocent as this.

"Put this on." He shrugged out of his jacket and handed it to me.

"I couldn't. What about you? Then you'll be cold."

"I'll be fine. I'm a big guy." He held it up, not taking no for an answer. I turned and let him help me slide into it.

It was huge. And warm. And it smelled like him—sandalwood, spice, and the crisp, clean scent of the icy fresh air outside. I almost groaned out loud but managed to refrain.

"Thank you. Freezing to death was becoming a real concern."

"Not on my watch. You're going to be home and safe before you know it."

Chapter 2
Spencer

Lucy Darlington.

Damn, she was gorgeous. She always had been. Soft, wavy hair the color of butterscotch and big brown eyes. We were the same age and often sat next to each other in school. I'd always had a thing for her, but we were total opposites. She was all about good grades, lots of activities, and going to college. She was an artist; I remember watching her draw in art class, mesmerized by the beauty she filled our assignments with. All I had cared about was fixing cars to race with my brothers. I never gave a shit about school, except for seeing her there.

I've toyed with the idea of asking her out on and off throughout the years, but I never found the right time. One of us was usually unavailable whenever the thought crossed my mind. Plus, what would someone like her do with a man like me? She was a children's book author and illustrator, and I rebuilt cars and drove a tow truck. We were still opposites.

I made quick work of hooking up her car, frowning when the snow started falling again in earnest. The road was iced over and slippery beneath my boots. I hurried back to the truck and climbed inside with a shiver. The temperature was dropping at an alarming rate.

"It's coming down hard again. Do you still live at the Honeybrook?" Her grandparents owned The Honeybrook Inn. Word was that she lived in the forest behind the main building in one of the cabins they rented out.

"Yeah. Will we be able to make it there?" Her gorgeous eyes drifted away from mine toward the snowfall outside the windshield. "It's getting bad."

"Bad? It's gone well beyond bad now. It's downright disrespectful out here. But we haven't failed yet." I patted the dashboard, questioning whom I was trying to reassure—her or myself, or maybe the truck. The road was slick; I almost slipped on the pavement as I walked back to the cab.

"Are you hungry?" She asked, gesturing to the bag of tacos.

I peered through the windshield at the mass of white flurries swirling in the glare of my headlights.

We were losing visibility fast. With the icy road conditions, I wondered if we should spend the night right here in the truck.

"Not anymore," I admitted, suddenly too on edge to even think about food.

"Oh damn. I knew it. We're in trouble, aren't we? I should have stayed at home. I'm so sorry. You would be way closer to town if you hadn't stopped to help me." The tremor in her voice chased my trepidations away. I was determined to get her home safe.

"No. Please don't apologize to me, Lucy. Would you rather be alone out here? No way, your car would have been buried by morning with you inside of it. Then what? Anything could happen to you out here."

"Okay, what's done is done, right? No more apologies. At least we know we won't get buried in this truck. It's too tall for that."

"Right. We'll be okay. I'll make sure of it." I pulled away from the side of the road, trying not to let my doubts show. It was dumping snow like crazy, and even my truck had limitations.

So far, so good. We were driving steady, and I let out a relieved breath as we slowly but surely headed up the road. Silence descended between us as I shifted my focus to keeping us on the road.

The quiet was unnerving during a storm like this. The chill in the air and the heavy snowfall muffled the usual ambient sounds. It was a phenomenon unlike any other. It felt strange, like wearing earmuffs or being trapped in an echo chamber, and I hated it. But the combination of silence and darkness was what truly unsettled me. This is why I was headed home instead of cruising around all night looking for people to help, like my brothers and father were doing right now.

"It's not snowing anymore," she whispered, then pointed wildly out the front window. "Look out, Spencer, I think there's ice and sleet up ahead."

With white knuckles, I held on to the steering wheel, trying to keep us steady. I could hardly see the road in front of us anymore, the flurries were so thick. The truck skid, sliding back and forth in a chaotic zig-zag as I gripped the wheel tight, fighting to keep control.

My heart flew into my throat as the light from the headlights bounced dangerously close to the metal guardrail. I knew this part of the road well; if we went over the side, there would be nothing but a vertical drop into darkness and death.

Lucy squealed, grabbing onto the handle above the door and bracing her other small hand on the dashboard.

My muscles burned as I turned the truck away from the rail, scraping the side as I straightened it out and got us back on the road. I drove a few feet until we were away from the edge and slowed to a stop, throwing it into park as I tried to get myself under control.

"Shit." I huffed out the breath I was involuntarily holding. "That was—I don't know what that was, but I don't want to do it again."

"We almost went over the side, Spencer." Her voice was small and frightened. Her hand drifted to the console between us and I took it, interlocking our fingers. I had no words of comfort to give.

Rationally, I knew we were safe for the moment but still, I glanced out the window to confirm we were on the road and not falling to our death.

"Maybe we should just stay right here," she suggested.

"We can't stay here. It's still too dangerous. We can go to my family's cabin and wait the storm out there. We're close."

"I don't know—"

I turned to her with earnest eyes. "Listen, you've known me since kindergarten, Lucy. My hands will be kept to myself the entire time. I swear it on the memory of my mother. You'll be safe with me."

"Oh no, Spencer. That's not what I was saying. I didn't mean to imply—"

I had to get hold of myself. She was already frightened. She didn't need me to add to it. I took a deep breath, then slowly let it out, hoping to release some of my fear along with it so I could be reassuring.

"I wasn't trying to imply you were implying anything," I teased, trying desperately to lighten the mood. I didn't like that she was scared—possibly of me. "Remember Charlotte? My little sister?"

She nodded. "She's nice. I love her books." Charlotte was a famous murder mystery author. She'd moved back to the area not that long ago.

"Yeah, well, women have to think about shit like this no matter who they're with, and I want you to know you'll be safe with me. I promise."

"I trust you. I've known you forever, and you've already saved my life tonight."

"Yeah, that was too close. We should get off the road until the storm clears. We're going to be fine. Try not to worry; I drive out here, in weather like this, all the time, okay?"

"Okay, let's go. And, hey, I do trust you, I meant it when I said it." She grabbed my hand, holding it as her eyes pleaded with me to believe her. "I sat behind or beside you in almost every class since kindergarten, okay? Please don't think I was trying to besmirch your character."

She trusted me. Her saying those words in that sweet voice of hers hit me straight in the heart. I refused to let her down; we'd be okay no matter what I had to do to make us that way.

"I would never accuse you of besmirching anything, Lucy."

"Well, good." She blurted right before her nervous laughter filled the truck's cab. "Thank you.

"We'll have to drive about a quarter mile up the road."

"Shit," she mumbled.

"Yeah, I'll go slow. We can make it." I don't know who I was trying to reassure more, her or myself.

"You got this, Spencer." She let go of the door handle with a sheepish smile. "Let's go. The sooner we get off this road, the better. Right?"

"Right," I muttered, turning the wheel to ease back onto the road.

She let out a low scream when we hydroplaned again. "God, I'm so sorry. I'm such a wimp. You don't need to listen to me carrying on like this."

"It's okay. If I didn't have to focus, I'd be screaming too."

"You're so nice."

I didn't answer.

I didn't want to freak her out, especially since screaming seemed like a good idea. Panic was setting in again. This entire night was my worst nightmare coming to life. I stuck to the day shift for a reason. The dark was not my friend.

We headed up the road, what felt like inch by inch. It was slow-going, but I finally reached the turn-off leading to my family's cabin. The only trouble was that this was an old mountain road, unpaved and rugged. I doubted we would make it all the way.

I drove about a mile or so, then had to stop. A tree had fallen, blocking the road.

I dragged a hand over my face, then rested my forehead against the steering wheel to catch my breath and bring my heart rate down to normal. It was about to beat straight out of my chest. My worry for her and my unease about our situation had taken hold of me again for a moment, but I brushed it aside and sat up.

"We have to walk the rest of the way, Lucy," I whispered, my stomach pitching as I took in what she was wearing. Yeah, she had my jacket on, but beyond that, she was in Converse sneakers and jeans. I knew this was not the time or the place, but I couldn't help but notice how they clung to each of her gorgeous curves. She had gotten wet when I picked her up earlier. She was shivering despite the heat blasting from the vents, and it would only get worse once we got outside. How would she make it the rest of the way to the cabin?

But on the plus side, she was tiny. I could carry her

over my shoulder if I had to, and then we could build a fire and warm up once we reached the cabin.

"Crap." Fear filled her eyes as she shook her head from side to side. "I'm not dressed for this. Tonight will go down as the stupidest decision I've made in my entire life. Even worse than when I tried out for the cheer squad and broke my arm. Or the tragic bangs I had all through eighth grade."

"I remember that. You whacked me in the head with that cast every time you had to grab something out of your backpack. It stuck straight out to the side at first, right?"

"Not quite straight out. But yeah, it was bad enough. Anyway, I'm a walking disaster." She let out a huge sigh and sank into her seat. "It's been a life-long affliction."

I turned, grinning at her sideways. "You are no such thing."

"Thanks for saying that." Her shoulders shrugged as she grinned back and tilted her head to meet my eyes. "And thanks again for carrying my backpack and books around for me. What a pain in the ass, right?"

Wrong. I loved being able to help her out.

She'd always been a little bit quirky, and I enjoyed her silly sense of humor in class. However, she was so shy around me that it was hard to get her to talk back then. I used to wonder why, but I gradually chalked it up to our different personalities. We had never been part of the same crowd. She was too good for a guy like me.

But she had the most stunning eyes I'd ever seen, big and brown with gold flecks. And more than that, I could tell she was unequivocally herself.

Nowadays, I loved running into her around town, and more and more, I find myself noticing when she isn't around. I would have a soft spot for her forever.

"No. I was happy to do it. And for the record, you were cute with those bangs." Too bad she'd been too shy to talk to me back then, I would have asked her out and maybe we would be together in an entirely different scenario right now.

We both flinched as a burst of hail pelted the windshield.

I held my breath, then let it out in a relieved sigh when it passed.

"What the heck is going on tonight?" She shook her fist at the widow. "Damn you, Skip McFadden!"

"When has that idiot ever been right about a forecast? He better not show his face in town ever again; that's all I have to say. We should get moving before it starts dumping snow again."

"Okay." She inhaled sharply. "I'm ready."

I wrapped my scarf around my neck and tucked it into my hoodie before I thought better of it and took it off to offer it to her. "Here, I want you to take this too."

She shook her head. "No way. I'm already wearing your coat. I'm the ill-prepared one tonight. You shouldn't be the one to suffer for it."

"You're also a lot smaller than me. I can take the cold better."

Her eyes filled with tears. "I'll never be able to thank you enough."

"Hey, I'm just glad I found you." I wrapped the scarf around her neck, tucking the ends into the coat and zipping it up all the way before brushing her tears away with my thumbs. "We'll be okay. I promise you, Lucy."

Her big eyes met mine as I gathered her hair in my hand, freeing it from the scarf to flow over her shoulders in a silken river of honey-colored waves.

She looked good in my clothes, even though they swamped her. For some reason, taking care of her this way felt right. A small smirk played at the corner of my mouth when she unconsciously buried her nose in the scarf and inhaled.

"Ready?"

"Almost." She put the taco bag in her backpack purse and slipped it on. "We're eating these fucking tacos when we get there, Spencer."

My lips shifted up in a grin. "Hell yes, we are.

Come on. Get out on my side so I can help you. I don't want you to fall." I opened my door, stepped down, and held my arms up to help her hop down. I steadied her when her feet slipped on icy ground, freezing in place when I realized I had inadvertently grabbed two handfuls of her rounded hips.

"Off to a good start already," she muttered.

I quickly removed my hands, wrapping my palm around the back of my neck as I glanced away.

"I might end up having to carry you at some point. I don't know how deep the snow will be when we get close."

Her eyes widened as she peered up at me with a trusting smile.

"Are you okay with that?" I asked her.

"Yes." Her cheeks pinkened as she gave me a jerky nod. "I mean, yeah, I'm fine with whatever gets us to safety. Of course it's okay."

"Good, alright. Let's move out. We can do this, Lucy. One foot in front of the other, that's it. Follow behind me, and I'll clear a path for you. If it gets to be too much, please tell me."

"Okay. I'll tell you." I was not convinced.

"I'm serious. Promise me. If you get home and lose your little toes to frostbite, I'll never live it down, and I'm not into being the town pariah."

She laughed. "Well, now I'll actually tell you. I was going to try to tough it out."

"I had a feeling." I grabbed my flashlight, pocketed my keys, and shut and locked the door.

I lifted her over the tree, then took her hand and the lead, stretching my arm behind myself for her to follow me. I didn't want to risk us getting separated.

The cabin was close, but the road was treacherous even on a good day. It was a private road, and we kept it graveled, but bad weather made it hard to navigate. The ice and snow made it significantly worse, not to mention the darkness pressing in on every side. Lucy was counting on me getting us to the cabin in one piece. And I'd be damned if I let anything happen to her.

Chapter 3
Lucy

I shivered as the cold went straight down the neck of Spencer's coat, chilling me to the bone. The scarf had slid out of place, but my hands were just too cold to fix it. It was big, the neckline gaped, and my hoodie was insufficient to keep the icy draft out.

One foot in front of the other. I could do this.

If—*when*—I got home, I would have a good talking to with myself. Maybe I'd never leave the house again unless it was the middle of summer. I mean, as far as I knew, Oregon had never had a surprise summer snowstorm.

The spiky tops of the evergreens stood tall like dark sentries against the night sky, and as it sometimes does here, the hail only lasted a minute. The snow, however, had decided to return to the party and was now falling in fat blobs, pelting us in the head as we trudged through the crispy, ice-covered mud.

I could tell there was a road here, but it was a mess —slippery in spots and covered with fallen branches and wet leaves.

The light from Spencer's flashlight was almost worse than being in the pitch dark. It created shadows that my overactive imagination ran wild with.

I was scared out of my mind.

I gripped Spencer's hand hard. I didn't want him to worry, so I kept my thoughts to myself. The idea of getting separated terrified me, so I held on tight.

The reassuring grip of his hand comforted me, but I was starting to doubt my ability to make it to his cabin without my feet freezing and falling off. My shoes were soaked and caked with mud, and the treads were packed with ice.

Like, I'd always wanted to hold his hand, but not like this. I couldn't even get a proper thrill out of it because I now knew what it felt like to be an ice cube, and I didn't like it one bit.

"Spencer," I called and tugged on his hand. I couldn't make it. I couldn't feel my feet anymore.

He stopped and turned. After one look at me, he raised his eyebrows. I nodded, and without a word, he picked me up and slung me over his shoulder.

I started making a quick mental list of every part of

my body he was touching so I could think about it later, like when I was alone in a bubble bath at home or whatever. But I stopped when I realized it was practically all of them, since I was plastered across his shoulder with my line of sight trained straight on his gorgeous ass.

His arm was banded around the back of my thighs right below my booty, and my breasts were flattened against his upper back as I held on to his waist and tried not to stare too hard at his spectacular butt as he walked.

This was a perilous, dangerous, freezing-cold situation, but my inner perv had come out anyway. My hair hung in my face, along with the scarf. Thankfully, it was still loosely wrapped because it was nice, and I'd hate for it to end up on the ground, especially since I had been trying to figure out a way to steal it to keep as a memento whenever we got to safety.

Wow, he was strong. It was almost effortless for him to lift me. His muscles flexed against my torso as he walked. And amazingly, he was warm, while I shook like a leaf inside his coat with my teeth chattering and nose running. I didn't even have it in me to care what I looked like. All I wanted was to be warm again.

"Thank you!" I shouted against his back.

I felt him nod against my waist. God, the side of my butt was right against his head and not how I used to picture it. Damn, back in high school, I used to dream of being close to him—being in his arms, sitting on his lap, and being pressed up against him. But it was never quite like this.

I quit watching his ass and switched to watching his sensible winter boots trudging across the snow-covered ground while silently vowing to repay him somehow.

Good lord, I owed him so much more than just a few freaking tacos.

"We're almost there," he yelled and shifted me higher. "I see it now."

"Thank god," I mumbled, grabbing onto his belt loops to keep myself steady.

His arm tightened around the back of my thighs as he picked up his pace, and shamefully, I shivered from more than the cold as his big hand gripped the side of my leg below my hip to keep me steady.

There was no doubt in my mind that this relentless, lingering crush I still had on him would humiliate me by the time this was over. I was going to die from exposure or embarrassment. Which one would feel worse as it happened, I did not yet know.

I knew I couldn't keep my feelings hidden for however long we were stuck together out here. My face was like an open book on a good day. Add the fact that I was freezing my ass off in wet clothes and scared out of my mind to the vast array of emotions I was currently experiencing, and he'd know my entire life story by the time we were able to go home. I mean, if we didn't freeze to death in all this damn freaking snow, that was.

"We're here." The words were muffled against my body, but I heard them.

Carefully, he set me down. I tried not to pass out as I slid down the front of his hard body, my nipples hardening as they dragged down his chest.

Holy crap, this was amazing. Could a person be hot and freeze their ass off at the same time? Someone should come out and study that phenomenon, I would be the perfect test subject because I know my cheeks were in flames right now.

He cleared his throat. "So, we're here," he said in a deep rumble.

I looked up, disoriented, as I took in the charming, covered porch of the cutest log cabin I'd ever seen.

It was A-frame and built with rough-hewn logs. Pine and fir trees surrounded it, their branches heavy with snow and sparkling in the beam of Spencer's flashlight. Two heavy wooden rocking chairs sat on one end of the porch with a sturdy table between them. Sitting out here on a nice day would be so peaceful, maybe with a cup of coffee and a good book.

I turned to see the moonlight breaking through the

canopy of trees, bathing everything in a silvery glow. I was freezing and all out of sorts, like I was waking up from a dream.

"Wow," I muttered. "This place is adorable. Like a fairytale cabin. Are there three bears inside? Please tell me there's porridge. I'm starving, and I think the tacos are smashed."

His smiling eyes met mine. "God, I hope not. But one time, when we were kids, Charlotte and I discovered a bunch of bats up in the loft. That was not fun. Let's get inside." He pulled his keys from his front pocket and unlocked the door.

I shivered, suddenly realizing precisely how cold I was as I stepped inside. "I'm a Lucy cube. I think I'm frozen solid." My bones ached from the cold.

"No worries. This place has a huge fireplace. We're going to be fine. There are also forks, plates, and everything else we'll need for the tacos. No worries."

I shut the door behind me, frowning in disappointment when he flicked the light switch, but nothing happened. "Damn, the power is out. What are we going to do?"

He flicked on a lantern that was on a hook by the door. "Always be prepared. That's what my dad always says. And don't worry, there are plenty of batteries."

"I love it here already. Thank god we made it." I

was so grateful to be here that I was ready to sink down to my knees and kiss the floor.

"My hands are like ice." He blew on them as his eyes drifted around the room, taking stock of what was here.

"Let me help." I attempted to wrap my hands around his, but they were huge.

"Thanks."

I let him go, taking a step back to look around.

The bottom level was a wide-open space. A kitchen was straight ahead on the far side of the cabin, a staircase to the right, and a fireplace to the left. Two large windows flanked the front door, and a comfy-looking couch sat on one side of the massive stone fireplace, with two chairs on the other. The walls and floors were, of course, wooden. Nothing but pine and whatever else kind of wood as far as the eye could see. It was adorable.

"Take off your jacket and try to get comfortable. I'll build a fire, and then we can make a plan." He was already by the fireplace, stacking wood on the open grate. He was competent, in charge, and taking care of me like no man had ever done before, not even my father. It was sexy as hell.

"Let me know what I can do to help."

"Listen, before you do anything else, call or text your mom or change your voicemail to say you're with me and where we are if you don't have a signal. She'll worry about you. Our phones might die while we're up here if the power doesn't come back on."

"Oh god. I'll never live any of her antics down, will I?"

"I mean—she loves you. That's a good thing." He bustled around the space, locating more battery-powered lanterns and flameless candles and turning them on one by one. It felt good to be out of the dark.

"Yeah, but being the parent volunteer—slash—chaperone—slash—room parent for every single school year of my life was—*gah!*—it was just too much. She is the quintessential helicopter mother."

"I just—"

"Oh god. I'm being insensitive. I'm so sorry." Spencer's mom passed away when we were in first grade. My heart broke for the little boy I used to know. I felt like an insensitive idiot for accidentally bringing it up.

"No apologies. That wasn't what I was getting at. You're pale, and your nose is red. We need to warm you up."

"Maybe we need to get out of these wet clothes." I joked to cover the fact that I was about to lose it. I fumbled with my backpack purse as I dug for my phone to change my message as he suggested.

He let out a chuckle. "We really should. There's a

dresser in the alcove over there near the stairs. It's full of clothes. They might smell like stale mothballs and old dryer sheets, but they'll be clean. Help yourself to whatever looks warm."

I watched, entranced, as he kicked off his boots and tossed his flannel shirt, followed by a thermal henley, toward the coat stand in the corner. He missed, and they landed with a wet splat on the floor.

I shrugged off his jacket and my wet hoodie and hung them up, toeing off my Converse, then bending to peel off my wet socks. "I really should rethink my cold-weather attire. I need to do better." My teeth chattered as if to emphasize my point as I hurried to grab his clothes and hang them up for him.

I spun to see him standing there in nothing but a soaking wet, skin-tight, and see-through white T-shirt and a pair of jeans that clung to every inch of his muscular thighs and—other parts. My eyes bugged out as I took him in.

"Thanks for hanging that up. And hey, don't beat yourself up. No one expected this." He gestured to the window where we could see snow dumping like crazy. We were lucky we got to the cabin when we did, or we would have been in real trouble. "Once the fire gets going, you'll feel so much better. Then we can figure everything out, okay?"

"Sounds good. I can't thank you enough, Spencer."

"We got this. We will be fine. I promise you."

"Okay." He was so sure we would be fine that I had no choice but to believe him.

His hands reached the hem of his shirt and lifted it. I gasped when it flew into the corner before he turned to the fireplace and knelt to shove some kindling between the logs on the metal rack. "You don't have to pick up after me. I'll get it when I'm done."

"Holy crap," I mumbled under my breath because so many muscles had entered my field of vision, and I couldn't quite believe what I was seeing.

He was huge. His back was like a broad, muscular wall. It took all I had not to stare at him. I mean, I was quite literally freezing my ass off and had to pause to take in the view before I went in search of dry clothes and possibly a towel.

Wow—like serious wow.

I shook my head and turned toward the dresser, blindly making my way across the room. I dared not turn back to look at him again because I was in real danger of a swoon.

He'd rescued me from my car, carried me through the snow, and was now unwittingly putting on a show that had come straight out of one of my better high-school fantasies.

Stuck in the snow with Spencer Cassidy?

Yes, please. Don't mind if I do.

I set my purse and cell on the dresser and took out the taco bag, frowning when I saw they were smushed. Damn.

"Good news! I located the matches." Excitedly, he strode across the room to join me at the dresser. "We have a fire. Hopefully, the power will come back on tomorrow. If not, we have more firewood in a shed behind the cabin. We're good for tonight. It's too dark to grab more right now."

"Oh yeah. Do not go out there. Being alone in a cabin in the woods is not my idea of a good time."

"And being outside in a dark snowstorm is not mine. We'll be okay, I promise, Lucy. I won't let anything happen to you." He held his hand out.

I took it with a smile, letting the heat of his big, warm palm infuse me with some of his strength. A tingle shot through me as his thumb stroked the back of my hand in a soothing motion.

"I won't let anything happen to you either, Spencer. Team Snowbound, that's us."

His gaze seared me with intent and promise. "I like it. Team Snowbound."

My stomach growled. "Smashed tacos and no porridge. What are we going to do? At least there are no bears. Or bats, oh my god."

"I'll grab what we need from the kitchen." He took the bag from the dresser. "You're not going to starve on my watch.

"All I can think of now is burying myself under one million blankets. I'm so cold."

"About that." Eyes filled with concern met mine. "We used to have bunk beds in the loft, but all that's up there now is the air mattress I used last time I was here, and it has a hole in it. We never stay here all together anymore, so my dad got rid of them. He's going to buy a bed for up there but hasn't gotten around to it. I thought we could grab all the blankets and pillows and pull the sofa bed out."

He reached out, almost touching my face with the back of his hand, but he pulled away before making contact. "I don't like how pale you are. It looks like your bones are about to shiver right out of your body. You don't look so good, Lucy. I'm worried about you."

"I don't feel that good. And I agree. I'm going to steal every bit of body heat that comes out of you, Spencer. You're about to have a Lucy-shaped barnacle attached to you all night. I hope that's okay."

"It's totally okay. You're going to be fine." He let out a relieved sigh. "You can trust me. I swear—"

I put a hand on his arm, needing the contact. "I know I can, and I do, and I appreciate you saying it again."

He reached around me and grabbed a pair of pink and black striped thermal pajamas from the open top drawer. "These are Charlotte's. They should fit you."

"Thanks." I took them and watched as he dug out a T-shirt and a pair of gray sweatpants for himself.

What was hotter? Skin-tight wet jeans or gray sweats? Maybe I was the one not to be trusted tonight.

"Go into the bathroom and get changed. I'll take care of everything out here. There should be towels to dry your hair, new toothbrushes in the drawer, whatever you need. But I'm not sure about hot water." He pointed to a door next to the stairs that led up to the loft space. "Wait a second, here you go, take this." He gave me his lantern. "There should also be one on a hook by the door."

I took it in my trembling hand. "Okay. Thanks."

I set the lantern from Spencer on the counter and switched on the one on. My face in the mirror spooked me. I looked terrible. I was pale, with dark circles beneath my eyes. I wasn't wearing much makeup since my date was a last-minute thing, and I hadn't had time to go all out, so at least I didn't have huge streaks of mascara and eyeliner to deal with. I wiped what remained with the hem of my shirt and cringed at my reflection. It's true, I was tired, but this was ridiculous. I turned on the tap, crossing my fingers that there would be hot water, but there was none to be had.

I sat on the toilet seat to peel off my jeans, staring longingly at the massive old-fashioned cast-iron tub. I would do anything for a steaming hot bath right now, and this one was just like my mother's. It was longer than I was, so I could fit head to toe if I wanted to.

Hurriedly, I stripped off the rest of my wet clothes and hung them over the shower curtain rod to dry. Looking around, I found a towel on a hook by the shower. It smelled clean, like fabric softener and fresh air. The pajamas smelled good, too. He must have been joking about the mothballs, thank goodness. I dried my damp body, slipped into his sister Charlotte's PJs, and then wrapped my hair in the towel.

When I returned to the main living space, I found him with an armful of blankets. He had pulled out the couch bed and lined the top and sides with pillows, creating a cozy nest in front of the fireplace. My heart melted, even though my body was still as cold as ice. He quickly added the last few blankets to the top and waved me over.

"Come on. Let's get you warm."

"That looks so cozy." I stepped toward him, then hesitated, nervously twisting the hem of my pajama top between my trembling fingers.

I, Lucy Darlington, was effectively living out my lifelong dream, and I could hardly believe it.

Snowed in inside of a romantic rustic cabin, about to be nestled down in a cozy blanket fort beside a roaring fireplace...

With Spencer freaking Cassidy.

Chapter 4
Lucy

The reality of our situation hit me as I took everything in—his earnest smile, the blazing fire. He had taken care of me tonight. What would have happened if he hadn't spotted me?

Immediately, I burst into tears as delayed panic shot through my body. "Oh my god, Spencer. I could be dead in my car right now. You saved my life."

"Hey." He threw back the covers and beckoned me closer. "Shh, come on. It's going to be okay. Let's get warm. We're inside, and we're safe. We have a fire, a stack of blankets, and tacos." He gestured to a bowl on the end table beside the couch. "I also have these." He held out a pair of fluffy pink socks, dangling them between us. A half-grin slid across his face as he tried to cheer me up.

I swiped my hand beneath my eyes and nodded. "I'm sorry. I'm being dramatic and silly."

"No, you aren't. Tonight was scary. Cry as much as you need to. Let it all out. I won't judge you. Maybe I'll even cry with you," he teased gently. "Come on." He reached out his other hand, and I took it, allowing him to pull me gently toward the couch bed. "Your hands are like ice. I'm going to help you put on your socks, okay?"

"Thank you. I don't understand how you're so warm right now."

"You're tiny." He shrugged. "I'm huge. Plus, I've just always run hot, I guess. I hardly ever get cold."

I scooted to the corner of the couch and leaned into a pile of pillows. "Well, I'm always cold. I'm shaking worse than my mother's Chihuahua right now. But don't worry, I won't try to bite you or hump your leg—well, your ankle. Buster is too small to reach leg level."

He chuckled as he knelt on the bed across from me. "That's good to know."

I cringed as I felt my face get hot. "I'll stop talking now." Or maybe I should say more. The blush was warming me up. Or was it having his hands on me that had me all hot and bothered?

His big palm encircled my ankle, and he carefully slid the sock onto my foot.

"Thanks..." I said, exhaling and watching in rapt

attention as he tended to my other foot. The only thing that could make this moment better would be if I could actually feel my feet.

"Your feet really are freezing." He observed with a frown as he rubbed them between his hands.

"I know. I can't feel my toes anymore. What if I get gangrene and have to get some amputated? Will I get a discount on pedicures? Could that be a macabre silver lining to this situation?"

Smiling eyes met mine. "Stop being hilarious and cute. I can't take it."

I glanced at him from beneath my lashes, then quickly looked away. "Aw, I was aiming for tempting and gorgeous, dang it."

I inhaled a soft gasp.

I was flirting with him.

Me, nerdy arty, weirdo Lucy was flirting with Sexy-Spencer.

Maybe the near-death experience had cleared away some of my shyness. Or maybe I was just sick of regretting how I had always been too nervous to really talk to him. Carpe Diem, I decided I was going to make the most of this.

"If that's what you're aiming for, you succeeded." His eyes remained on me when I looked up. "I wasn't sure if I was allowed to flirt with you tonight. Can I?"

"Trust your instincts, Spencer," I replied with a

grin, thrilled beyond words that he'd returned my flirting. "You're already irresistible. I was a snowbound damsel, and you saved me. You carried me to a cabin in the woods, built a fire, and are currently warming my feet. Are we in a fairy tale right now? Are you secretly a prince?"

"A prince who works on cars and drives a tow truck? I don't think so." He released my feet, dragging a hand down his face as his cheeks turned pink. "Anyway, I think I can help, I mean with your feet. Can I try?"

I burst out laughing. "You're already helping me, Spencer."

He lifted his shirt and pulled my feet close, hugging them in his arms and pressing them against his abs.

I squeezed my eyes shut as I resisted the temptation to feel him up with my toes. God, ever since high school, I'd been such a freaky little perv when it came to him.

I peeked at him from the corner of my eye. "You are literally a human space heater. That feels so much better. I was tempted to stick them in the fire for a minute there."

Our eyes met and held as heat flared between us—not just between his abs and my feet—real heat. His eyes blazed into mine. I was not imagining this. I sank into the moment, letting myself feel it, making a memory of it so I wouldn't doubt it later when my insecurities rose and tried to make me let it go.

He cleared his throat, breaking the moment. "So. Uh..."

"Yeah. I mean—yeah. Um..."

"Should we eat the tacos?" he suggested.

"Good thinking." I unwrapped my hair and tossed the towel in the corner with his wet shirt. "I'll pick that up tomorrow, and your shirt too. It's the least I can do."

"Thanks." He reached for the bowl. "You were right. They're pretty beat up. But they still taste good. I snuck a bite when you were in the bathroom."

I grabbed the second fork from the bowl and took a taste, tipping my head back with a groan. "Delicious. I was on the verge of becoming hangry. You don't deserve to be stuck with me in that mood. It can get pretty ugly. I feel like we earned these."

He let out a chuckle. "We sure did. That was an interesting drive, to say the least."

"Interesting, yeah. You got that right."

We finished eating the tacos in no time. As we ate, the fire took the icy cold edge off the space, and I relaxed a bit.

"I'll take that."

"Thanks." I passed him the bowl, and he put it on the table.

He slid down and turned to his side. "I'll repeat it. You're safe with me, I'm warm, and you're welcome to share it."

Warm?

No.

He was hot.

Spencer was the sexiest man I'd seen in my entire life. A laugh shot out of me as I contemplated the ridiculousness of this situation. Earlier tonight, I'd been on a ten-minute date from hell, and now I was up close and forced proximity-personal with my secret high school crush. *Go me.*

I slid beneath the covers, resting my head on the pillow beside his. His arm stretched over my head, and his body heat beckoned me like a beacon. I turned to face him, biting my lip as I tried to think of something normal to say. Being normal was hard for me under average circumstances, and I worried about what would come out of my mouth when I was still one-quarter freaked out, okay three-quarters. Lying to myself was a bad habit I had yet to quit.

"I went on a date tonight. It was terrible," I blurted. "The only good thing about it was the tacos."

Holy crap, what's wrong with me? Too much information, anyone?

His body tensed, eyes growing sharp. "Do I know

him?" He asked without missing a beat or making me feel awkward. "Is he your boyfriend?"

"No, well, maybe. I mean, no, he's not my boyfriend, and maybe you know him." I shook my head, trying to get my nervous energy out of it so I could make sense. "He lives in town but is not a local; he's new. He invited me out at the last minute, and I stupidly said yes. Then, when I got there, he asked why I wasn't dressed up, like hair, makeup, heels—he told me he expected more from a date and that my butt was too big for my jeans. So I left. I stormed from the table in a huge huff and ordered the to-go taco platter because fuck that guy."

"First of all, he asked you out at the last minute and expected—what exactly? It's Taco Time. What the hell? That place is a dump. The food is great, but it's a total dive."

"Exactly! That's what I said. Well, that's the nicest thing I said, anyway."

"Good for you." His eyes raked me up and down before gifting me with a lazy smile. "Don't take crap from anyone. And second, Lucy, sweetheart, any man who doesn't appreciate how stunningly gorgeous you are—and I'm including your amazing ass in this statement—is a fucking idiot who doesn't deserve one single moment of your time."

I sank into the bed as all the air left my body. My

eyes got huge as my brain rattled around in my head, trying to take in what he had just said to me.

He threw back the covers and stood up, startling me. "It's time."

"What?" My eyes darted to him with concern. "Wait, are you leaving? Where would you go?"

"I'm not going anywhere except to the other side of the bed. Get into my spot. It's warm."

"Oh, okay. You had me worried for a second. That you—"

"What, that I expect hair and makeup formality when we're in the weirdest situation ever? That you have to put on a show and not be a real person with fears and concerns?"

I rolled into his spot, sinking into his leftover warmth with a thankful sigh as I pulled the covers up to my chin. As discretely as I could, I inhaled a deep breath, taking in the scent he'd left behind—it was heavenly, crisp, and clean, like sandalwood and fresh air. My thawed-out toes curled into the mattress as I fought the urge to pinch myself to make sure I wasn't dreaming. Why did he have to smell so good?

"Maybe. I don't know. I never know how to act around people. I've known you forever, but we don't know each other well enough not to make this awkward. Does that make sense?"

"I understand what you mean, but we've already

moved past awkward tonight. Let's get comfortable and try to relax so we can sleep. I promise not to judge you for being emotional or scared. I guess what I'm trying to say is that I don't expect any formality, and I hope you feel the same way."

"I do feel the same. You've definitely seen me at my worst. Like nose running, smeared makeup, spiraling into a freakout, crying worst. And let's not even get into what my hair must look like right now."

"Likewise, you saw me get nervous in my truck. I was scared too, and also worried that I would end up failing us both. And full disclosure, you were in the bathroom when I sent my dad a panicked help-me SOS text—which, sadly, did not go through."

"I guess we are trauma-bonded for life now."

"We are. And we're going to be okay." He circled the bed and then climbed in next to me. "How are your feet feeling?"

"So much better. I can feel my toes now, and there is no pain. That's probably a good sign, right?"

"Yup. But you'll be paying full price next time you get them painted that pretty shade of pink."

Chapter 5
Spencer

The wind howled outside. Although I knew we were safe in the cabin, the noises coming from outside were still unnerving. I inhaled deeply and slowly exhaled, trying to set my fears aside so I could be strong for Lucy. I was used to it here, used to the creaks and groans this cabin always made as it settled, to the brush of the branches against the sloped roof, and the sound of the wind through the trees.

The couch bed was small, not even queen-sized, and I was a big guy. Although we weren't touching, I could feel her as if she were pressed against me. Her energy was palpable. She was still afraid, I could tell.

I had always liked her too much for my own good. There was something special about her, and this was the perfect opportunity to get to know her better.

"How long do you think we'll be stuck here?" She

faced me on her side, hands tucked under her cheek with the covers pulled up to her chin. I almost couldn't believe she was really here. "It sounds like it's getting worse out there."

"Probably not long. I sent texts to my family, but if they don't go through soon, there's a radio somewhere around here. And if that doesn't work, I can hike out to the truck and use that one. And if all that fails, my dad will figure it out."

"I've always liked your dad."

"He's easy to like."

"He helped my mom a lot after my dad took off, along with my grandparents. He's a good guy."

Our parents had been friends of a sort; they went to school together. Her dad was a CPA who worked on the accounts for Cassidy's Automotive. Now he was somewhere a few towns over with his third or fourth wife. I could never understand how he could just leave Lucy like that.

"Yeah, he knows what raising kids on your own is like. It isn't easy."

"She was not good after he left. She's a little better now. She's still overprotective, though. She's going to freak out so hard when I get home. I'm not looking forward to that."

"You're her only child. I guess it's understandable. But I'm sorry you have to bear the weight of it."

"And you're one of six. That must be so fun."

"Most of the time it is. They can get nosy, though."

"Look at us, having a casual, and dare I say it, almost normal conversation?"

"We've broken the ice."

"Nice pun, Spencer. *Ice.* I like it."

I watched her smile at me, and for the first time this evening, I believed we would be okay.

The wind blew through the evergreen bushes planted near the porch, scratching against the cabin. If I hadn't spent most of my life up here, I would have felt as nervous as Lucy looked. Her eyes widened as she stared at the uncovered window.

"It's just the wind. Don't worry."

"Okay, are you sure?"

I nodded. "So, what's his name?" I asked about her date to distract her. I also wanted to know what kind of moron would treat her so poorly.

She deserved so much better, someone who knew what he had when he was with her and would treat her accordingly. Plus, what kind of asshole talks to a woman like that? Someone should teach him some fucking manners.

"Huh?" She turned to face me. "Oh, you mean my date from hell. Well, you won't believe this, but I met Skipper McFadden at Taco Time for dinner."

I burst out laughing. "Are you serious?" Immediately, I felt relief. I felt bad for her that she had to deal with a fool like him. But I felt great; that narcissistic asshole was not a threat. He was a pompous dick when he was on TV reporting the weather, so even if he went crawling to her on his knees full of apologies, he was no competition.

"We matched one of the dating apps I'm on. We've been texting for the last few days, and he invited me out tonight for tacos. I was bored, so I said yes. He assured me we would only get a light dusting of snow and that I'd be fine driving down to Sweetbriar to meet him for dinner. In retrospect, I think he was probably just trying to get into my pants. *'Come on, Lucy. The weather is fine, and I'll buy you some tacos.'*" She mocked his on-air voice, and I chuckled at how accurate she was. "As if that would be all it took. I'm not that easy, Spencer."

"The dumb fuck said it on air, too—insisting we were only going to get a light dusting of snow." I threw a hand out, gesturing to the window where the snow was still falling in earnest. "Unbelievable. And as for the rest, you were right—fuck that guy. He doesn't deserve you. You're much too beautiful, funny, kind-hearted—I could go on, but you get my point. You don't belong with a man like that."

"Oh." I grinned as her cheeks turned pink. "You're

sweet. I always knew you were nice. But I didn't know you were sweet too. I like it."

I leaned closer. My voice was rough and low, gritty with lust that I couldn't manage to completely hide. "Then I'll be sure to keep it up."

"Like I said earlier." She sucked in a slow breath as our eyes locked. "Trust your instincts."

Something hit the side of the cabin with a dull thud, and she flinched, shaking the whole bed and snapping us both back to reality.

"What the hell was that? Bigfoot? A serial killer? Good lord, it's demons. I know it. We need salt, Spencer. Is there any salt in the kitchen? I've been binge-watching *Supernatural* and—"

Her mood changed so fast it was as if she got whiplash. It was probably for the best, even if she was about to freak out. It wouldn't be right to take things too far tonight.

What had I been thinking?

I could not allow myself to go too far.

This was Lucy Darlington.

I would not be flirting, flattering, or fucking her in any way, shape or form while we were here.

I was currently in bed with sweet, good-girl Lucy Darlington and I needed to maintain control over myself.

But god damn it, how I wanted her to be *my* good girl...

Knock that shit off.

"We don't need salt." I sat up, squinting into the dark outside the window. "It's just the wind. We're okay. It was probably a fallen branch."

She sat up as well, leaning into my side to follow my gaze. "Are you sure," she whispered, clutching my arm.

Her soft breasts pressed against my bicep, and all the blood in my body rushed south. I grabbed a pillow, shoving it in my lap to hide the fact that I was now hard for her.

So what if I kissed her?

My hands shook from fighting the urge to pull her close.

Just one kiss. What could it hurt?

I knew it would be good. She had the prettiest lips. Soft and full. Pouty and a deep rose-petal pink—

No.

"I'm sure." I struggled to speak, my voice strained as I tried to hide my racing thoughts about her and me, about being alone together, and the fact that we were attracted to each other and—

Fucking stop it.

Think of something to say and quit looking at her chest.

I slammed my eyes shut and blurted out the first thing that came to mind. "I don't think *Supernatural* is a good choice for entertainment when your mind jumps to demons before the weather. Also, Remy and those ranger guys are full of it."

"He's seen some shit out here, Spencer. You know it's true."

"Maybe a quarter of it is true," I conceded, subtly leaning away from her.

She smelled too good to be this close. I couldn't take it. I had to find a way to share this bed with her. It was hard enough without her touching me.

"This forest is full of scary shit and a whole bunch of trouble. I can't believe I hike out here sometimes. No more hiking. Never again. And why don't you guys have curtains on these freaking windows? Anyone could be out there watching us. Plotting and making nefarious plans to roast us in that fireplace for dinner. You won't fit in there, Spencer. But I will—"

"We don't need curtains," I insisted. "No one comes out here—"

"Oh my god, shh." She put a finger on my lips, and I groaned out loud. Lucky for me, she was too freaked out to notice what she was doing to me. "Do you hear that," she hissed.

My eyes snapped back to the window again. It was

more of the same—wind, snow, dark. There was nothing there but a bunch of trees and bad weather.

"Snow weighs branches down, and ice makes them break," I explained. "Then the wind blows it all around. You know this. You've seen it happen with your own eyes. I promise you we're safe in here. But if it makes you feel better. I locked the door. No one is getting in here, I swear."

We were in two different realities right now. While I fought my baser instincts and tried to regain my composure, she believed we were about to become victims of whatever paranormal entity her racing thoughts conjured up.

I would have laughed if I wasn't trying my best to channel every shred of dignity and discipline I could muster so I could help her snap out of what was clearly the beginnings of a panic attack.

"Locks won't stop demons, Spencer. Or freaking ghosts. Or Bigfoot. We need salt! Oh my god, I thought I was okay. For a few minutes, I actually believed I could sleep tonight. But everything is hitting me now. I'm pretty sure I'm coming unhinged. The wheels are coming off, Spencer. I might freak out for real."

She clutched the covers at her chin in a white knuckled grip.

"You will not come unhinged, not while I'm here. This is anxiety. This is fear talking. Will looking out the window help? Then you'll see where the sounds are coming from."

"Hell no. It's dark out there. It's dark in here, too. Well, it's dim, and the fire is making freaky shadows. I'm going to stop thinking. I have all kinds of bad feelings but will ignore them all. La la la, I'm okay. You're okay, it's ohhh kay—"

"Lucy. Sweetheart, stop. Take a deep breath for me."

I watched her inhale. She shook her head and held her breath, slamming her eyes shut against her rising panic.

I leaned into her, putting my face directly in her line of sight, lightly touching my forehead to hers. "Open your eyes. Let that breath out and tell me what you see."

She exhaled in a whoosh. "I see you," she breathed.

"Good." I took her hands and held them against my chest above my heart. "What do you feel?"

"You." Her voice was a whisper. "And your heartbeat."

"Good girl. Take another breath for me."

She inhaled, and this time, it was nice and easy.

"What do you hear?"

"You, Spencer."

"That's right. Me. I'm here, and I will not let anything happen to you. I promise you."

"Thank you," she whispered. "I'm so sorry. I was trying so hard to be okay."

"No apologies, remember? And it's okay not to be okay."

"No apologies. Right, I'm sorry. Damn it. I take it back. I'm not sorry."

"I have a confession," I interrupted. "Maybe it will make you feel better."

Her gorgeous eyes met mine. "Tell me. Please."

"I hate the dark. I can't stand the silence when the snow falls, and everything outside is quiet and still. I was afraid, too, Lucy. I started heading back to my place late. My drive home was not going well. Then I found you, and helping you gave me a sense of purpose. Making sure you were safe kept me from losing control. So, thank you."

"You're welcome," she murmured. "I'm glad I accidentally helped you. Thank you for letting me know."

I gently touched the tip of her nose with my fingertip and then lightly kissed her forehead. "But don't tell anyone else."

She smiled. It was tremulous and faded fast, but it was real. "I swear, Spencer, I won't say a word. You're right. We're okay. We're not sliding around in the snow at risk of hypothermia or attacks from a serial killer. I'm keeping all my toes, and we don't need demon salt. Like you said, we're safe, right? We're in this sofa bed together, warm and alive. Yeah, it's dark, and the weather is crazy, but at least we're not alone. I could be in my car right now, huddled under the floor mats and that gross blanket I keep forgetting to take inside to wash. Now we have two secrets together, don't we?"

"I guess we do. No one will find out about you and Skipper McFadden, and you won't tell anyone about my thing."

She twisted her fingers over lips like turning a key in a lock. "I already forgot about it. Spencer Cassidy is not afraid of the dark. I know nothing."

"Ha, thanks."

"I feel better. Maybe I can fall asleep after all."

"Same."

"Spencer?" she whispered.

"Yeah?"

"Will you hold my hand?"

"Absolutely. And Lucy?"

"Yeah?"

I took her hand and kissed the back of it. "I need this as much as you do."

Chapter 6
Spencer

I woke to light shining through the window, and at some point as we slept, Lucy had draped herself across my chest as if she were always meant to be right here. Not one inch of her sweet little body was not touching me. So much for holding hands—she had her legs wrapped around mine, her full breasts were flattened against my chest, and her arm was bent, with her hand in my hair. I vaguely remember her running her fingers through it while she slept, but I couldn't be sure since I was most likely at least half asleep when it happened. Or maybe this was a dream, and I hadn't really woken up yet.

Slamming my eyes shut, I fought against getting hard, thankful that, by some miracle, I hadn't woken up that way. She was warm and soft, and I had no idea how to get her off me when every part of my being wanted to pull her even closer, to get lost in her and forget we were stuck here in an uncertain situation.

I glanced out the window and saw nothing but white. Snow covered the trees, and the sky glowed brightly from its reflection. It was almost as beautiful as Lucy.

Shit. We would probably be stuck here for a while. But would that really be such a bad thing?

I watched her sleep, trying to convince myself I wasn't a creep for staring. But where else could I look when she filled my entire field of vision? Not to mention how gorgeous she looked while asleep had occupied every single one of my thoughts. Her already beautiful features had softened. I was fascinated by the delicate bridge of her nose and the shadow her lashes cast on her high cheekbones. Her lips were full and pink, and I found myself wishing I could lean in and kiss her awake.

Carefully, I removed my hands from her back, clenching them into fists at my sides. I wanted her bad. To be fair, I had always wanted her, and that was the problem. But the timing had never been right. Now, it seemed we had nothing but time.

There was a hitch in her breath as she stirred in her sleep. Was she waking up?

I had no idea what time it was, but it felt early.

"Spencer?" Her soft murmur interrupted my conflicting thoughts, and I tried to gather my wits.

"Good morning."

"Oh God. I'm sorr—*Gah!* I won't say it." She rolled away and pulled the covers over her head. "You really are like a space heater. Obviously, I couldn't resist. Where are my manners? Good Morning. This is not at all awkward. Oh my god."

"Everything is okay. You're right. I am warm and completely irresistible," I teased. "And didn't we talk about not being awkward with each other last night?"

She rolled to face me, and a sheepish smile slid across her face as she lowered the covers. "Yeah, I can't help it though. I'm a mess."

"You're not a mess. You kept me warm last night, just like a little blanket. Seriously though, how are you feeling?"

She met my eyes with a clear-eyed gaze. She looked better. The tinge of panic I'd kept seeing last night was gone. "So much better now that I've gotten some sleep. I haven't had much in the last few weeks."

"I'm glad." I took her in. Studying her face to make sure she wasn't trying to put up a brave front while wondering if it was okay to ask her why she hadn't been able to sleep.

But I kept getting stuck on how pretty she was in the morning light. Her hair was adorably tangled, a mass of light brown waves the color of butterscotch. I wanted to sink my hands in it, bury my face in it. I wanted too much, too soon, and didn't know where to put these out-of-control feelings.

"I was all over you. I was kidding when I said I'd be on you like a barnacle, but, um, I, well, is that okay? Like, do you have a girlfriend? I haven't heard about you dating anyone in the town lore, but I haven't been out and about as much at all. I've been on a tight deadline until a couple of days ago."

"Ahh, I know all about deadlines from Charlotte. So you've been mainlining coffee and wearing nothing but pajamas? Is that why you haven't been sleeping?" My sister, Charlotte, was an author of murder mysteries, and Lucy wrote and illustrated children's books. Larry the Llama was almost as famous as Pete the Cat.

"Something like that. I finally showered and changed the day before yesterday. And then I wasted my first free day on that stupid-ass, Skip McFadden."

"At least there were tacos," I joked. "And no. I don't have a girlfriend."

She looked me dead in the eye. "There was one unexpected silver lining to this whole debacle, and it was not the tacos, Spencer. It's you."

I didn't answer. I couldn't say anything because the urge to grab her and kiss the hell out of her overwhelmed me and I thought it best to just keep quiet.

"Anyway." She coughed lightly, breaking the mood we'd stumbled into. "I would commit murder for a cup of coffee right now."

"You won't need to. We have a French press, a fire, running water, and coffee. There's even powdered coffee creamer or Yoo-hoo if you prefer that."

"Are you serious right now? I was mourning the loss of my morning shower, but coffee would make anything almost better."

"You could take a cold shower, or we could heat some water for sponge baths."

Her face lit up, and I grinned widely at her.

"Is there food here?"

"I checked last night when you were in the bathroom. There's plenty of food in the freezer, the pantry is stocked, and the stove is gas, so we can cook whatever we want. We'd be okay if we had to stay here for a month. My dad went all out last time he shopped for this place."

"So, you're telling me we're not going to starve to death. And I won't go into caffeine withdrawal?"

"Nope, there are three kinds of coffee. Tea too. And some Oreos that I'm considering having for breakfast."

"Oreos are my favorite, especially with high-quality black coffee." She sat up and looked out the window. "Holy crap, Spencer! Have you looked outside yet?"

"Yeah, it definitely snowed all night."

"We're in the middle of a snowpocalypse. This hasn't happened in a few years."

"Yeah, and now I have two reasons to knock Skip McFadden around whenever I see him," I muttered.

"Two?" She appeared confused for a moment, but then her face turned bright red, and she smiled. "I don't know what it says about me, but I love the idea that you're willing to knock him around for me."

"I'm pretty sure I'd do anything for you." Damn, did that count as flirting?

"After yesterday, the feeling is mutual." Her blush intensified, and she dipped her head to look at me from behind the fall of her hair. She was so fucking beautiful it almost hurt to look at her.

The mood was back.

"Stay put. I'm going to add a log to the fire and start the coffee." I quickly got up and headed to the fireplace.

I wasn't ready for the mood, and it wasn't right to pursue her here, anyway. We were stuck together, and putting that kind of pressure on her would be wrong. I knew this last night, but it got buried beneath my rabid attraction to her.

I placed another log in the fire and moved to the kitchen.

It was too early to put my feelings on the line. She had said to trust my instincts, but what if they were wrong?

"I'll make lunch today," she offered. "I love cooking."

"You've got yourself a deal."

"How long do we have before the food in the freezer goes bad?"

"We keep a cup of frozen water in there with a dime on top just in case the power goes out when no one is around. The dime was still on top last night, so we should be safe for the next few days as long as we keep the door closed as much as possible. We can always pack it with snow if needed to make it last longer."

"Would it be stupid to drink our coffee outside on the porch? I know it will be cold. But it's gorgeous out there."

I turned and saw her standing in front of the window, fingertips pressed against the glass. She was short, but her legs appeared long, maybe because her waist was so tiny, like a little hourglass.

She had soft curves, full, lush breasts and an ass that came straight out of a fantasy. And although I couldn't see it right now with her back turned, she had a dimple when she smiled. For years, that dimple drove me crazy, especially because it appeared when she smiled, and I always loved it more than I should when she smiled at me.

"No, we have a portable fire pit and plenty of winter clothes. Sometimes, I come up here alone to think. I always sit on the porch with my coffee."

She crossed the room to stand at the counter, watching me gather the coffee supplies. "It was the first thing I thought of when I saw those rocking chairs last night. It's so peaceful here."

I could see her here with me, somewhere in the future. Rocking in the chairs my dad built, drinking coffee, at peace, happy together...

I gritted my teeth and reminded myself that we were in an extreme circumstance. Our emotions, including our attraction to each other, were running high, and the worst thing I could do was act on them now, no matter what she said about trusting my instincts. *I* couldn't trust my instincts right now, and that alone should be enough to hold me back.

"This is my favorite place," I told her as I scooped coffee into the French press and deliberately kept my eyes on the task at hand instead of her sweetly smiling face.

She was unlike any woman I'd ever known. When we were kids, I knew she was an open book—she would say anything that popped into her head, and it was usually spot-on, witty, and hilarious. She was well-liked, sweet, and kind to everyone, and it seemed like she hadn't grown out of that. There was no artifice to her.

With Lucy, what you see is what you get. I found it as amazing now as I did back then. I was finally old enough to fully appreciate it this time. Now, I wouldn't get hung up on my own insecurities and let her get away.

I *was* good enough for her. Things like getting good grades and what crowd you hung around with were meaningless in the real world. Spending time with her here made me realize we weren't quite so opposite anymore. The more we talked, the more I believed I could have a chance with her.

"I can see why. I'm already in love with the place. Thank you for sharing it with me." She was luminous. Gorgeous. I could get lost in her eyes. The kindness and sincerity that radiated from her stunned me almost into silence.

"Of course." I blinked, refocusing my gaze as I tried to think of something to say. Taking part in this conversation would be a good idea. But, damn, she was doing my head in with her early morning cuteness. "How do you take your coffee?" I managed to ask.

"I like it black if it's good."

"Me too." The similarities between us were stacking up one by one, almost as if this were meant to happen. Yeah, this was only how we took our coffee, but I couldn't help but smile.

"How strong do you want it?"

"Spencer, I want it to show up on a drug test."

Unable to fight it, I burst out laughing. "Are you the perfect woman?"

She was. At least I was beginning to believe she could be perfect for me.

"Of course I am! Don't you know that by now?" Her mouth quirked with humor. She was smiling, bantering as if she hadn't had a traumatic night, and, most importantly, she was relaxed. The contrast was like night and day, and I was relieved. "So, how should we spend the day? Given how it looks outside, it seems we won't be going anywhere anytime soon."

"No, it's pretty packed in. I'm just hoping I don't have to dig my way to the shed to grab more wood for the fire."

"I'll help you if you do," she sweetly offered. "I swear I won't start a snowball fight, and I'm definitely not crossing my fingers behind my back."

"I'm glad you're feeling better. I was worried about you last night."

"After my dad left, my normal, everyday anxiety went into overdrive, and I would get panic attacks. It hasn't happened in a long time, years, in fact. Last night was overwhelming. I was exhausted and over-stimulated, and it was just too much. I'm sorr—" She bit her lip before finishing the apology.

"Hey, it's okay. I'm glad I could be there for you."

"Me too. You pulled me through it, and I appreciate it. I owe you a taco dinner. Me. You. Taco Time. As soon as we get out of here."

"Are you asking me out?" I winked at her. "I accept."

"Yeah, maybe I am. Is that okay?"

"Trust your instincts, Lucy." I turned her previous words back on her, hoping she'd be the one to take the lead. As long as we couldn't leave, being the one to make the first move felt wrong to me.

"Ahh, you are a clever man." Her glance was bemused as she regarded me with open curiosity.

"I try." I poured her coffee and then slid the steaming mug across the counter. "Taste this."

After blowing on it, she took a careful sip and then tilted her head back with a sigh. "It's perfect." She grinned at me. "Aside from how we got here, it almost feels like a vacation now. Is it weird to think that way?"

"Nope. I always try to make the best of things. Let's change into warm clothes and go outside. We can check our phones and figure out what to do next."

"Sounds like a solid plan. I hope you don't mind sharing your Oreos with me."

"What's mine is yours."

Chapter 7
Lucy

After rummaging through the dresser, I was fully clothed in fancy skiwear and sturdy winter boots, courtesy of his sister. I also owed Charlotte some tacos or whatever else she preferred since, judging by the amount of snow out here, I would probably end up wearing every stitch of clothing she kept here before we could go back home.

Snow blanketed the ground, dusting the porch steps and weighing down the branches of the evergreens. It was everywhere, covering everything in fat, fluffy piles.

The steam from the coffee mingled with the crisp morning air as I rocked in my chair, wrapped in a quilt, with one foot resting on the porch rail. I was right; I knew it would be peaceful out here as well as incredibly beautiful. No wonder this was Spencer's favorite place.

We had come out here together, but he returned inside after we realized our phones still had no signals. He was trying to contact his dad with the radio. I almost didn't care if he reached him or not. Now that I was safe and knew I would be fine, I felt selfishly happy to be here.

I hoped my mother was okay, but it was a relief not to have to answer a million questions about where I'd been, where I was, and what I was currently doing. I loved her, but sometimes, she drove me crazy. She respected my working hours, but beyond that, it was open season on my time, and I felt terrible that I felt this way. I was not good at setting boundaries when it came to her. She needed me.

The desire for a day or two of peace and quiet surprisingly outweighed my feelings of embarrassment for waking up on top of him. I squeezed my eyes shut at the memory, trying to forget how it felt to be pressed against his gorgeous, hard body, how it felt to have his big thigh between mine and my hand in his hair. I only wished I could remember how we ended up in that position. I'd bet money that sleepy Lucy had enjoyed herself.

The sound of the door opening and closing interrupted my quiet reverie. I turned to smile at Spencer expectantly, deliberately keeping my eyes trained on his face and no lower.

"I got through to my dad. Power is out in Honeybrook Hollow and all the villages north. Sweetbriar is fine. The storm knocked down a few trees and made a mess, just like I thought. The turn-off to the cabin and most of the surrounding roads are completely blocked, including the section of the highway that runs through Honeybrook Hollow. A few of the big pines went down. Crews are working on it now. But the road to this cabin is not a priority since it's just us out here, and they know we're okay. He'll head out to your mom's place, let her know what's going on, and make sure she's okay and has what she needs. We could hike out if you'd like, but the snow is deep."

"Maybe we should stay here?"

"That's what I think."

"Between your dad and my grandparents, my mom will be fine. Don't you think?"

"Yes, she'll be fine, Lucy."

Shamefully, my eyes lit up, and I smiled, giving myself away. "So I don't have to worry about her then?"

Understanding eyes met mine. "No, he said he'll check on her. You have nothing to worry about; he will also check on your grandparents and ask if your house has any damage."

I owed his dad so many tacos now, too. When I get

home, I might throw a Taco Tuesday thank you party to express my gratitude in one fell swoop.

"Thank you so much. What can I do to help? We need to gather more wood, right? Anything else?"

"Nothing except add finally buying a generator for this place to the to-do list. But that is a chore for another day." He sat in the rocking chair next to mine, crossing an ankle over his knee as he settled in with his cup of coffee and the bag of Oreos.

"Right? I even have one at my place."

"I do, too. Do you really live at the Honeybrook now?"

His sideways smile warmed me up. He was so handsome in the early morning sunshine. The bright light reflecting off the snow shone in his eyes, making them sparkle like sapphire lightning.

God, I was losing it so bad over him. I had to force myself to keep up my half of the conversation. Concentrating was going to be difficult when he looked this good. Maybe I shouldn't look at him at all. Would that be rude? I decided against it because it would definitely be weird.

"Uh, yeah. I moved into one of the cabins a few years ago. It's perfect: one bedroom, one bathroom, cozy, and not too far from civilization. I can order from the Inn's restaurant if I don't want to cook. They have everything now: a spa, a gift shop, even a little coffee hut near the road. You'd love it there. It's secluded like this place."

My grandparents had owned an inn called The Honeybrook for over forty years. It was busy year-round as Mt. Hood was one of the most popular destinations for skiers worldwide.

"I stop there for coffee way more than I want to admit." His mouth slid into a smirk, and he held his mug toward me for a toast. "It's almost as good as my coffee."

That did it. I clinked my mug to his, vowing to spend all of my mornings at Mystic Mocha from now on. Then, I'd be sure to run into him more often.

"The coffee is amazing," I agreed. "It rivals Violet's Café in Sweetbriar, but I will never say that publicly, so don't even try to quote me." Violet's coffee shop was widely regarded as the best coffee shop in the area.

"I won't say a word." He passed me an Oreo from the bag on his lap. "You forgot about these."

"Gimme!" He chuckled as I eagerly reached for one. Our hands brushed as he placed it into my palm, and my entire body heated. Immediately, I looked away, dunking the cookie in my coffee to cover the fact that he was getting to me. "Yum. Best breakfast ever."

"Agree. Nothing better."

"Uh, what do we have in there for lunch?" I asked inanely.

"Mostly pantry stuff and frozen dinners. There's no meat, or I would have dug out the grill."

"In this weather?"

His sideways glance was adorable and don't get me started on his grin.

"Nothing stops a Cassidy man from grilling, Lucy. Rain or shine."

At this moment, it became clear. Forget about dying of exposure. This hopeless crush I had on him was going to do me in. I was in real danger of making a fool of myself over him.

"Are you a meat group foodie?" I teased. It felt good to flirt with him. He wasn't constantly pushing for more than I was ready to give. It was as if he had an innate sense of how far to go. Or maybe he was just a gentleman or even an expert flirt.

"Yes. I like to cook. It's relaxing. And I love to bake, too. I have a chocolate chip cookie recipe I've been perfecting. Those are my favorite."

"I know about your cookies. I've tried one, and they're amazing. You entered the harvest festival bake-off with those cookies and won last year. It was quite scandalous around The Honeybrook."

"Yeah, I can't believe I beat your grandma." His lips twitched with suppressed laughter. "My father was mortified."

"Ehh, she got over it. Especially since she kept her

streak going in every other category." My grandma had won every ribbon in every Honeybrook Hollow bake-off competition since before I was born.

The day he beat her was another day of many when I had regretted not talking to him.

"So she's not pissed at me?"

"Nope, "You can't win 'em all," she said. She thought it was hilarious that everyone was tiptoeing around her like she would be upset."

"So, then, if I picked you up for a date, she won't run me off the property?" There was an invitation in the depths of his eyes. One I was determined to finally take.

I sighed, delighted at the turn in our conversation. "No. You'll be safe. Are you asking?" My eyes hovered on his, relieved when a look of flirty indulgence crossed his face, and he smiled at me.

Not to be dramatic, but I was starting to believe if I didn't get to see his smile at least once a day, I would die of withdrawal.

"You asked me first last night, remember? For tacos." He teased, leaning forward with his elbows on his knees to face me fully.

"You're right." I inhaled slowly trying to be cool and not throw myself at him. "That I did."

"But I have to say, I wish I had been the one to ask first; it should have been me. I wanted to so many times over the years. I've actually thought about asking you out for a long time."

My mind whirled as I replayed every interaction we'd ever had. So many missed opportunities.

I sat there blinking. Blinking and thinking. Pondering and perplexed.

I needed words, and I needed to respond, but my mind was currently shorting out because he had blown it.

What if I'd been more open?

Flirtier?

More freaking self-confident?

"I take it back." Realizing this was my time to make up for every lost chance I had to go out with him, I followed my heart and blurted, "It never happened. I never asked you out. Not a hint, not a peep, not a word. Tacos what? Tacos, who?"

Featherlike smile lines crinkled at the corners of his eyes. "God, you're cute. You know what? I almost asked you to senior prom. I wish I had. Maybe things would be different now—I don't know. I haven't had the best luck with relationships."

I may have just died. My heart had literally seized in my chest.

The ghost of Lucy was now in charge of her body, and she was confused as hell.

I mean, what the heck?

I could have been living in an alternate reality right now. One where I could have avoided years of bad dates with dumbass losers.

And Spencer? He thought that *I* could have made a difference in his dating life?

What the in the everloving dreamstate fresh hell was going on right now?

Was this cabin the portal to hot guy Narnia? Was I stuck in the sexiest hallucination ever? Was I about to have a dream come true?

"Why didn't you?" I squeaked out, trying to wrap my head around the beautiful, amazing, mind-boggling words that were coming out of his mouth.

"My dad told me not to. Your mom wouldn't let you date. Isn't that right?"

"Ugh, yes." I threw myself back in my chair, flinching when it hit the wall behind me. I felt myself shrink, like the girl who was always stuck at home. My mother was always too afraid I would get hurt or be peer pressured into doing something bad, like get pregnant or do drugs. Because of this fear, I could never do anything with my friends. Damn it. "No, my mom wouldn't let me date until I turned eighteen, and I'm so thrilled you know about that," I muttered.

"I'm sorry, Lucy—I never told anyone, I swear. He didn't want me to get you into trouble or cause a fight with her."

My freaking mother. Damn it. She only had herself to blame for her lack of grandchildren, forcing me to date idiots when, for all these years, I could have had Spencer. She was going to hear about this when I got home. For the love of—

Enough.

Getting lost in what could have been was stupid when what was happening *right now* was way more important.

Focus.

"I saw you there," I told him, for lack of a better segue into another topic. "At prom, I mean."

"I went with my friends. I couldn't bring myself to ask anyone else." His voice broke with huskiness. Did he have any idea how sexy he sounded? "I didn't want to. I was too disappointed that I couldn't go with you."

Holy crap. Holy freaking crap, crap, crap.

Forget my Man Ban. I was now on the Get Spencer Cassidy Plan with a side quest to find a rhyming name to call it.

This was happening.

"So did I," I stammered as tingles of awareness shot through my body. "I went with my friends too, I mean."

"I should have asked you to dance." His expression stilled and grew serious as our eyes locked on each other.

"I would have said yes," I murmured. Touched

beyond words that he was sharing this with me. "I would have loved to have danced with you."

"You've been frustrating me for years, Lucy."

"Me?" My eyebrows shot up in shock.

"Yeah, you." He laughed lightly. "You drew me that picture after my mom died. Do you remember that? You've been in my heart ever since."

"Oh, Spencer. Oh my god." I closed my eyes, letting the memory of that time in our childhood wash over me as I settled into the change this conversation was heading into.

"Is that too much?"

"No. I love it. I'm so glad you told me. I—I didn't know what to do. You were so sad, and I wanted to help you somehow. It was all I could think of. Drawing is what I always do when I have too many feelings and can't figure them out."

"You drew her," his whispered voice grew hesitant. Gone was the self-confident flirting of only a few seconds ago. "It was more *her* than any of our photographs in my house. I still have it."

My heart melted, turning over in my chest. I was thrilled because I already knew I wanted it all. Every emotion, every feeling, I wanted all the pieces of him.

Tears filled my eyes, but I refused to let them fall.

"I loved her, Spencer. She was my favorite teacher —ever. I'll never forget her."

His mom had taught first grade, and I was one of her students. It was the only year Spencer and I weren't in the same classroom. She was diagnosed with cancer near the end of the school year and passed away over the summer break. It shook our small community; everyone loved her. She was one of those people who spread sunshine wherever she went.

"I'll be her age soon, and it gets to me sometimes. I don't know why she crossed my mind right now." He let out a rueful sigh and my heart broke for him.

"I'm so sorry. Why does life have to be so unfair? She was a wonderful woman, and you deserved more time with her. You all did."

He looked away, frustrated. "I ruined the mood. We were talking about dating and prom and fun things and—"

I gaped at him, shocked. "You did no such thing. I'm sick of *moods*. I just want to be real for a change. What you said was real. It was honest. It was how you felt in the moment and I'm honored you told me. I loved it."

"What do you mean? Real?"

"I'm tired of small talk, aren't you?"

His brows flickered a little as he nodded. "Yeah. Everything is always a game, it seems."

"Good. I'm sick of dating apps and meetings in bars. I'm sick of playing games too. I'm also tired of seeing where things go while he's talking to five other women. If I see the letters WYD in a text one more goddamn time, I'll lose my mind. And I'll probably drop dead or end up in prison for murder if I get one more dick pick. I'm over it all."

"Tell me what you want." A look of determination settled on his face as he waited for my response.

"I want honesty. I do not want to be a hookup or a booty call ever again. I want to watch TV in bed on a Saturday night after going to dinner or for a walk in the park or whatever. I want good morning texts that lead to goodnight kisses. I don't want friends with benefits. I want friends with possibilities and intentions and real, honest-to-god feelings. I want—I think I want the impossible, and that's why I'm done with men and dating and putting myself out there. No more. I'm honored you told me how you feel about your mom because it made me feel something. Thank you for sharing that with me because it was real."

"You're welcome." He looked as if he were in shock.

I'd blown it. Obviously.

Ranting Lucy was really good at chasing men away. Only this time, there was nowhere for this one to go.

Chapter 8
Spencer

I sat there, frozen. That was everything I wanted, but I didn't say it. Mostly because I found myself wanting it with *her*. Each word that came out of her mouth made me want her more, and I didn't want to put pressure on the situation. If she didn't feel the same way about me, or as strongly as I did, it would get awkward between us really fast, and neither of us could escape. On the other hand, if we started something and it was good, that would be another kind of pressure.

I was torn.

A declaration like she'd made demanded reciprocity. Only an asshole would leave her hanging, and I would rather die than hurt her feelings.

"I'm processing." I finally said. I needed a moment to decide how to proceed.

"Oh god. I might die of embarrassment."

"Don't. Please. I—"

She got up and darted into the house, leaving her mug on the table between us.

I heard footsteps, followed by the slam of the bathroom door.

Shit.

I slid my mug next to hers on the table and ran into the cabin. "Lucy!"

"Forget I said anything." Her voice was muffled behind the heavy oak door.

"I don't want to forget it." I shouted, leaning my forehead against the door and pressing a palm against it. "I want to hear more. I want to know everything you're feeling because I feel it, too. But I'm feeling it specifically about *you*, and I don't want to—I'd say I didn't want to chase you away, but there's nowhere to go. That's the only reason why I hesitated."

The silence between us was deafening until I heard the snick of the lock disengaging, followed by the soft squeak of the door as she opened it. My breath caught in my throat, and I stepped back, hoping she would forgive me.

She stood there, studying my face as she swept a hand beneath her pretty brown eyes to brush her tears away.

"Really?" she asked. Her lower lip trembled, and my heart cracked open.

"Yeah." The possessive desperation in my voice shocked me. I needed her to understand where I was coming from.

"Good. I mean, I believe you. It makes sense. Maybe we should start trusting our instincts with each other."

I stepped closer, placing a hand on the doorframe above her head so I could lean in. "I'm sorry I hurt your feelings. I didn't mean to."

A tremulous smile unfurled across her mouth as her eyes met mine. "I have this horrible habit of saying too much, too soon. I can hardly blame you for needing a second to process it."

"No. It's not horrible. I love it. I'm done with games, too. I want to be real with you."

She bit her lip. "I would like that. I'm always holding something back and tired of it, Spencer. It's exhausting."

"Don't hold back with me. Please."

"Okay..." she breathed, her hand went to my chest, and I sucked in a sharp breath as goosebumps spiraled outward from the heat of her touch. I lowered my face to hers until our mouths were mere inches apart. The prolonged anticipation was almost too much for me. I sucked in a breath, wishing I knew why I was hesitating.

Time stopped whenever I was next to her. It always had.

Her head tilted to the side as she watched me, worrying that tempting lower lip between her teeth. Then her eyes drifted closed, she relaxed, and her lips parted. She was so small I could tuck her beneath my chin, hold her close, keep her warm, kiss those gorgeous lips, and never let her go…

"No," I blurted, coming to a decision I wasn't even aware I was making. "I shouldn't kiss you right now. It wouldn't be right."

"It wouldn't?" Her eyes flew open, eyebrows drawing down in confusion.

"We're in an extreme situation. We can't leave. I won't take advantage of you."

"That's gentlemanly." She removed her hand from my chest, reaching up to absentmindedly twirl a lock of hair around her finger. I knew it was a habit of hers; I'd seen her do it so many times back when we were in school together, and I'd always thought it was cute, damn it. I needed her to quit being so fucking cute.

"Yeah, that's me. A gentleman." I huffed a bitter laugh. I must be out of my mind. All the signals pointed to yes. She all but told me to kiss her.

Trust your instincts.

I couldn't take advantage of this situation. Stuck here. Nowhere to go. Damn it.

I was my father's son.

He raised me and my brothers to protect and respect women.

But I had wanted *this* particular woman for so damn long. Therefore, she was the *most* important woman to protect and respect. *Fucking logic.*

I stepped to the side, gesturing for her to lead the way into the living room.

"Should we get more wood?" She turned back to ask. There was a pensive glimmer in the shadow of her eyes as she studied my face. I'd confused her. Hell, I confused myself.

"Yes, but I'll get it. The snow is pretty deep."

"Oh. Sure." A brief look of hurt flashed across her face. "I'll just—see what's in the kitchen then. Keep the fire going. Make the bed. Take a sponge bath. Then maybe I'll make us some lunch."

"Sounds good. I'll be back." I grabbed my coat and bolted to the front door to let myself out, stopping short on the porch when I saw it was snowing again. "Damn it," I muttered as I stalked down the steps.

We couldn't go home even if we decided to make a break for it and hike to the main road. It wouldn't be safe for her; she would be knee-deep in snow and possibly waist-deep in some areas, and actually making it to the highway was unlikely. Our only hope would be that my dad or one of my brothers could reach us, but they were busy helping out in town.

When I reached the small woodshed at the back of the property, I pulled my phone from my pocket. There was no signal, and the battery was almost dead. I needed to talk to my father, one of my brothers, or Charlotte. I had too many conflicting feelings running through my mind to sort them out on my own.

Trip after trip of carrying armfuls of firewood to the porch didn't burn out the tension coursing through my body.

How would I ever be able to hold myself back from her?

There was no way to stall any longer. We had more than enough wood. I stood in the doorway, contemplating my next move as I tried not to stare too hard at Lucy in the kitchen.

She hadn't heard me come in. Her back was to me as she danced to whatever song she was humming.

I cleared my throat to get her attention. I could not watch her shake that gorgeous ass of hers for one more second.

"Hey!" A startled laugh burst out of her. "You were out there for a while. Did you get wood?" We both noticed the juvenile double entendre at the same time.

She covered her mouth with her hand to stifle her laughter.

It broke the tension that had drifted between us when I left the cabin.

"Yeah, I got it," I grinned. "It's piled up on the porch in the rack. I'll bring some of it in later. The snow is pretty deep back there, like I thought. And it's coming down again."

Her hair was piled on top of her head in a haphazard and completely gorgeous topknot. My dad's red plaid "Kiss the Cook" apron was tied around her waist, but most of all, the sight of her grinning at me as she stirred whatever was making this cabin smell so good in the pot was about to undo every vow I had made to myself not to start something while we were here.

She was fucking irresistible. She was the embodiment of everything I'd ever wanted my future to be, right there within arm's reach. I could not allow myself to fuck this up.

"Come here. Taste this." She dipped a spoon from the dish rack by the sink in the pot.

"It smells great." I rounded the kitchen island and took her hand in mine to raise the spoon to my mouth.

She inhaled sharply and her cheeks flushed that pretty shade of pink I was growing so fond of. Despite myself, I was pleased that my touch had affected her.

"Careful, it's hot."

I blew lightly, my gaze fixed on hers, before sliding the spoon into my mouth.

"Delicious." I watched the play of emotions on her face as a soft smile floated across her lips.

"It's chicken noodle soup," she murmured. "My grandma calls it cheater noodle soup—all frozen, canned, and carton ingredients. It's yummy, though. Are you hungry?"

"Starving. Oreos aren't the best breakfast. But sometimes I can't help myself." I rounded the island again and slid out of my jacket, placing it on one of the barstools at the counter.

She tilted her head toward the sink, and I nodded as she filled a glass with water and slid it across the counter.

"Thanks." I tipped it back and drained it in one long gulp.

"Anyway, about that—not being able to help ourselves, I mean. I thought about what you said—about not kissing me—and you're probably right."

My eyebrows shot up. If she agreed with me, it would make this so much easier. "Yeah?"

"Yeah. So, no kissing. We'll agree that it is forbidden. At least not until after we go home. Does that make you feel better about being stuck with me? No hurt or hard feelings, just a healthy appreciation of our situation and the smartest way to approach it."

She held her hand across the counter. My lips twitched. I tried not to laugh as I shook it. This was the weirdest deal I'd ever made. "Yes, I feel better. But at the same time, also, no, I do not. Calling it forbidden makes me want it more, just saying."

"I totally get that. It's like having naughty Oreos for breakfast." Laughter lit up her eyes. "I wanted that kiss, Spencer, I'm not going to lie. But, after I thought about it, your restraint impressed me. We're all alone in this gorgeous, snowy cabin. It's romantic; there's a cozy fire, a comfy couch, and two people who have apparently had secret little crushes on each other for years. And let's not forget about the elephant in the room: there is only one bed. We don't want to rush things; in fact, we shouldn't. It's the smart choice. We just need to find some non-sexy activities to do together to distract ourselves."

The thought crossed my mind that any activity, no matter what it was, would be sexy if I was doing it with Lucy. I was screwed, no matter what we did.

I took a glance out the window, hoping it had stopped snowing, but no. Fate was tempting the hell out of me today. I had to be strong.

"Non-sexy, huh?" I tried to relax, but her eyes were on me, and I felt the weight of her stare like a damn touch. "Well." I coughed, eyes darting to the cabinet by the fireplace, needing to look anywhere else so I didn't have to look at her. "We have a ridiculous amount of board games here, in that cabinet. Probably a few decks of cards, too. We could play games to distract ourselves."

"Sounds like fun. Oh! I found the liquor. Your dad buys the good stuff. I'm impressed. Maybe later we can drink amaretto sours and play poker. But I have to warn you, I cheat at cards."

Could she get any cuter? She cheats at cards and admits it, damn.

"Ahh, but is it really cheating if I know you're going to do it?"

"Hmm, I see your point. I made it part of the rules, didn't I?" Her head tilted to the side along with one side of her mouth in a sweet little smile.

Was she trying to flirt with me, or is this just how she was now? The Lucy I had known back in school would never be this bold. I liked it far too much, considering the circumstances.

"Something like that." I couldn't take much more of this.

"Well, if I cheat at poker, what else will I cheat at?" She made a kissy face at me. "Clearly, I'm not to be trusted around card games or your sexy lips."

"I didn't know you were such a troublemaker." An

embarrassing flush heated my cheeks. This was a side of Lucy I had no idea existed, and I was into it.

"I've been hiding behind my good girl rep for years, Spencer. Living the solitary, weirdo art girl life. Writing children's books and doing whatever my mother tells me."

I let out a short burst of air. I would have laughed and joked along with her, maybe flirted back—what could it hurt? But I was so turned on right now that I couldn't trust myself. Or maybe I should just kiss her and give us both what we wanted.

Something had gotten into her while I was outside. She knew how badly I wanted her, so that had to be it. My feelings had made her bold, but something in her words held me back.

She deserved more.

Even though my feelings were real, Lucy deserved more than I could offer her while we were here. We had endless hours to wait for the storm to pass and help to arrive. She deserved phone calls, dinner dates, flowers, and wine. Lucy was special, and she deserved to be treated as such.

She'd already told me about how that little shit Skipper McFadden had treated her. I refused to be one of the guys who had let her down.

"Right?" Finally finding some words, I answered,

"I'm the one to watch out for if reputation is the only consideration."

"Totally, you're—too much. You're so good-looking, so hot, everyone thinks so. You used to race cars with your brothers on the weekend, Spencer. You drove a motorcycle to school. All the girls wanted to date you. I was a nerdy mess back in high school."

My eyes raked her up and down. "You were never a mess, Lucy. And you sure as hell aren't one now."

"Ha, you must be joking. I'm an entire mess right now, and I'm wearing your sister's clothes."

"Most of that stuff is new. Charlotte hates packing, so she buys stuff to leave here. I'll pay her for it, and you can keep it. I don't want that thought in my head. Nice try, but it's not the turn off you thought it would be."

"The joke is on you." She waved the ladle around for emphasis. "I'm not trying to turn you off. I just have no filter. Are you ready to eat?"

"Yes. Is there anything I can do to help?"

"Nope. You're keeping us warm today, so I'll keep us fed. I got this."

Damn, flirty Lucy and her lack of a filter were going to kill me.

I should have just kissed her.

Chapter 9
Lucy

Knowing that Spencer Cassidy wanted to kiss me had done something to me. My self-confidence was soaring, my crush on him had exploded, and it was all I could do to keep myself from jumping across this counter and throwing myself in his lap to give us both what we wanted.

He had come in from gathering wood. His wind-blown hair was tousled, looking like I had just run my hands through it instead of the wind, and his broad chest heaved with exertion. The light flush in his cheeks was adorable, making me want to kiss him all over. From the kitchen window, I watched him go back and forth from the shed to the porch while making the soup. I could see how his biceps bulged even through his jacket, and the tense line of his jaw, as he worked.

Both would fuel my fantasies, probably for the rest of my life.

There was so much wood out there that he must have been avoiding coming back into the cabin.

But what did I know? I relied on central heating for warmth. Maybe we needed all that wood.

What I knew for sure now was that Spencer Cassidy wanted me, and it excited me in a way that had me floating on air.

When he first pulled away from me, I was hurt, but it only took a minute for me to understand him. I always knew Spencer was one of the good guys. Having a dad like his made it a given. Since my dad worked with his father, we were invited to all of Cassidy's Automotive employee barbecues, so I got to see what his family was like. Aside from my grandpa, I had never known how it felt to have respectful, gentlemanly, protective attention directed solely at me.

I felt safe with Spencer.

It was a revelation.

He looked tortured when he pulled away from me. Entirely and utterly *tortured*, there was no denying it— I saw what I saw. He was all Mr. Darcy with the hand flex about me, and I was into it. The mini-crush I had kept in the back of my mind for all these years suddenly morphed into something I wanted to fully explore immediately.

It felt like he wanted to protect me as much as he wanted to ravage me, and it was a turn-on like no other. But I could wait for the ravaging if it meant I could keep feeling this way.

After years of dating dick-pic-sending, non-committal, emotionally stunted boy-men, I was finally in the presence of a real man. A grown-up, adult man. A *good* man. And bonus: he couldn't get away.

Bring it on.

I ladled soup into bowls, buttered some bread, and then joined him at the table without any idea what on earth we could talk about when everything he said only served to put me more under his sexy spell.

He had scrambled my brain, rattled all my senses, and made me feel things that no man ever had, and I wanted him so bad right now.

But I also wanted to respect his wishes. I loved how he wanted to wait almost as much as I hated it. Ugh, damn him for being honorable and kind, and sexy and hot, and everything I ever wanted.

"This is confusing me," I blurted. I was frozen in thought, with my spoon halfway to my mouth. "I don't know what to talk about."

"I don't either. Except this soup is great." He set his spoon down and reached for the bread.

"Thanks. I'll be sure to tell my grandma it was a success."

A grin tipped one side of his mouth. "You're too cute. I can't look at you."

"Thanks?"

His eyes darted past me to the window. "Shit," he muttered. "It's white out there. Whiteout. Look."

I turned. "Oh snap." Static filled the air, and I jumped in my seat. "What the hell was that noise? And what the hell is up with all this damn freaking snow?"

"The radio." He stood, tearing across the room and up the stairs to the loft.

"Great. More good news will be forthcoming, I suppose," I muttered to myself. "Saved by the static." I mean, it was snowing again. What else did we need to know?

The mood that had risen between us was dead for now, which was probably for the best as I was beginning to have my doubts that we could keep off of each other if we had to stay here much longer.

I finished my soup, trying not to think about what would happen once we got home. Would this end? Would we go back to our "Hey, how are you?" interactions and forget all the magic that has happened since we got here? The thought of not seeing him after this hurt.

Being here felt like the beginning of something, and I was afraid to think of what it was. I'd gone from vowing to be done with dating and men to wanting it all back again with Spencer.

I wanted a chance to be happy, damn it. But now I found myself wanting it with him.

What if he was getting news that we could leave? I wasn't ready.

Was I being selfish by not thinking about my family and what they could potentially be going through in town?

Or was it finally my chance to have something for myself?

I wasn't worried about my mom. Her house could withstand any disaster that came her way. Her anxiety wouldn't allow her to be ill-prepared for anything. Whenever I finally made it out of this cabin and went to her place to prove to her I was still alive, she'd tell me everything that happened while I was gone, how she was right about all her paranoid safety-freak ways, and how I needed to stock my car and house with more cold weather supplies—which, obviously, was a fair point—over peppermint tea and her sugar-free sugar cookies, which I, much to her amused annoyance, referred to as imposter cookies.

I wasn't worried about my grandparents either. The Honeybrook would also be okay. It had stood proud for almost a hundred years, weathering every storm that had hit this area. However, they wouldn't lecture me about anything when I got home. We'd just crack open a few beers by the big fireplace in the lobby and rant about storms from the days of yore and yesteryear and how much snow we'd be cleaning up around the property for the next few months.

I guess I could worry about my four half-sisters—my dad was a player before and after my mother, and during, too—but I didn't like to think about him. They were all scrappy ladies and would be okay no matter what.

"No news. Or at least nothing we couldn't have guessed for ourselves." Spencer's voice startled me as his boot steps sounded across the wooden floor toward me. I dropped my spoon in the bowl with a clatter. I really had to stop zoning out like this.

"Is everything okay?"

"Yes, for the most part, everything happening in town is to be expected. The usual: power outages, icy roads, fallen trees, and people hunkering down. So far, it's nothing out of the ordinary. It's good that the schools are still on winter break."

"So we'll just hang out here and ride it out. Are our families okay then? And what about my mom?"

"Exactly. We stay put. Everyone is fine. Your mom is at the inn with your grandparents and sisters. They're making meals for the Honeybrook Action

Center as usual and keeping the road workers supplied with coffee and snacks."

"I wish I were there to help."

"Me too. They could use another tow truck. But it is what it is. And it's best if they don't have to worry about us."

"Okay, I agree. You're right."

"Also, I found this." He handed me an emergency radio with a hand crank. "We can listen to music if we can get a station to come in. And you can have some actual music to dance to in the kitchen."

"You saw that?" Luckily the cringe I just cringed was not fatal and I would live another day and probably find another way to embarrass myself again somehow.

"Sure did." His smile turned into a chuckle "You have some great moves, Darlington. Prom was definitely a missed opportunity," he teased, rejoining me at the table and taking a bite of his soup.

"Oh my god." Brushing my embarrassment aside, I started cranking it and then turned it on. "I know you don't like the quiet. This is amazing." It was staticky, but I smiled when "1999" by Prince came on. "How apropos; tomorrow is New Year's Eve. We can party like it's—what, 2099? We'll probably both be dead by then."

Dying didn't worry me. Stopping myself from jumping Spencer is what worried me. I slammed my eyes shut when the mental image of kissing him at midnight tomorrow popped into my head. Damn it—I wasn't supposed to be thinking about things like that—like how sexy he looked in his blue flannel shirt. He'd rolled the sleeves up while he was in the loft, and how kind of him it was to give me something new to lust over.

"What a cheerful thought." He chuckled. "Almost as macabre as your gangrene pedicure discount."

I huffed a sardonic laugh. "I used to think of myself as an optimist, but I've spent too much of my life searching for silver linings. Those days are over."

"I feel that, especially after my last relationship."

"Oh yeah?" My curiosity piqued, and I leaned forward, steepling my fingers beneath my chin. "Want to talk about it? I'm a great listener, and my advice is usually well received."

One of his eyebrows shot up as he weighed the question. "Do you want to talk about Skip McFadden? And why you agreed to go out with a tool like him?" He finally answered me, and I smiled, not missing the gentle sarcasm in his tone. Maybe he was bad at love too.

"Oh god no. But I have already told you everything there is to know about him. And I get you. For the sake of fairness, you can always ask me about my dad or my last two boyfriends, then we can really get into it."

"Are we foregoing our plans for board games and poker for twenty questions?" He countered.

"Or maybe truth or dare?" I boldly suggested.

"I never turn down a dare and I'm honest to a fault. Better be careful what you ask for."

Blood pounded in my brain, and I enjoyed a full-body shiver. For someone who wanted to wait to kiss me, he was sure flirting his ass off right now.

"You're perplexing me, Spencer. I think I like it. Mixed messages are fun when I know what you really want."

My stomach tingled as his gaze traveled over my face, deliberately not looking any lower. His jaw tightened with the effort, and I fought the temptation to provoke him into checking me out. His attraction was evident, and I hoped mine was too. Who was I trying to kid? I had never been able to hide my feelings; he knew how I felt. Turning down a sure thing must have been hard for him, and it only made me want him more. The irony was torturous.

"You're not shy anymore, are you?" His low, husky voice sent a thrill through me. "I could barely get you to talk to me back in school, and I don't see you around town enough these days to try—at least I never seem to see you when we're single at the same time." He paused, drawing his lower lip between his teeth as his eyes flicked down to my chest and back up. The look was so brief that I might have missed it if I hadn't been watching him so intently. "And Lucy, I would have tried."

"The shy little artist you used to know back in school is long gone." I tried to steady my voice, making sure not to sound flirty. However, it came out Marilyn Monroe breathy despite my effort. "Writing and drawing take up most of my time, and I don't go out much. If I had known how you felt, I would have made it a point to seek you out too."

Fuck being shy. What did it get me? He wanted me, and I wanted him and we both knew it. Plus, I had just survived some serious shit. I almost froze my ass off in my car—literally. I could do hard things. I was a woman who was now going to get what she wanted— and what I wanted was Spencer Freaking Cassidy.

The tension between us was so thick you could cut it as we sat watching each other. Anticipation, as heavy as the snowfall outside, flittered in the air between us. His hands wrapped around his mug, gripping it tightly as the muscles in his jaw twitched in frustration. Unfortunately, the natural conclusion of this interaction was not going to happen because, apparently, neither of us was willing to take advantage of the other.

Chapter 10
Spencer

Instead of playing truth or dare, as she suggested, we played Monopoly, which I previously thought was the least sexy game ever. But that was before I played it with Lucy.

I took a sip of my drink, watching as she blew on the dice before tossing them. She bit her lip as they rolled across the board, and I shut my eyes against the sight of where I wanted my mouth to be.

I set my glass on the table. Alcohol was a bad idea. While I wasn't drunk, I was definitely buzzing, and I needed every ounce of control I had.

She counted off her moves, and I huffed a laugh when she bought a hotel to add to Indiana Avenue.

"Your turn," she said, all smug, satisfied, and adorable as fuck, dancing in her chair as she placed the hotel on the board with a flourish.

"Proud of yourself, are you?" I grinned at her and tossed the dice.

"A little bit." She held her glass up for a toast. "Cheers to me!"

"Cheers, sweetheart." I clinked my glass to hers and took a sip. Not kissing her was getting harder and harder the more we played.

Currently, I was about to go bankrupt. I had to give up my ownership of Park Place to stay in the game. Lucy owned everything on the two cheap sides of the board, from Mediterranean Avenue to New York. At first, I wondered why she was so obsessed with buying them, but her strategy became apparent once she erected hotels on her sides of the board. I was screwed, and she showed no mercy. She was ruthless.

Every move she made got me hotter for her. I couldn't stand up, or she'd see the evidence of it. I had a Monopoly kink now, and it was all her fault.

Lucy was sexy as hell, but more importantly, I wasn't afraid to talk to her, to let her in. Maybe it was because I'd known her forever. She had gotten into my brain and heart before I'd become afraid of being hurt by a woman. She was hilarious, intelligent, stunning, and cute. She had all these different personality traits within one sexy little body, and I was enthralled.

Suggesting we avoid starting anything while we were here was the stupidest idea I'd ever had. All I wanted to do was swipe the game off the table and play with her in other, much more naked ways.

"It's your turn," she informed me with smug delight, her eyes shining with satisfaction. She was secure in the knowledge she was kicking my ass as she should be.

"I'm not sure there's a point anymore, Lucy. I can't win."

My admission of imminent defeat amused her. I could see it in her smile, but there was also something lazily seductive in her look.

"It's not over 'til it's over, Cassidy. Roll the dice."

"As you wish, Darlington." I shook the dice in my palm and tossed them on the table—snake eyes. I moved my piece—the car, obviously—two spaces. I had to go to jail, directly to jail. "Damn. This is not my night for games."

"Ooooooh! You're under arrest, Cassidy! No two hundred dollars for you. Maybe you'd like to sell off some more property." She gestured to her pile of Monopoly money, which was practically all of it. "I can afford it."

"You're killing me. Go. Roll the dice. Let's get this over with so you can lord it over me for the rest of the night."

She swiped the dice off the table and rolled. Jail.

"Ha! Now, who's the one in trouble?"

"Look at us, Spencer." She moved her piece next to mine. "We're stuck together in the game now, too. Isn't that interesting? Could it be fate trying to tell us something?" She slid her chair back with a squeak. "Roll 'em. I'll go fix us some more drinks."

"Thanks, but I'll take water. One more drink, and I'll be officially wasted."

"Good point. I'm a bit tipsy. Drunk Lucy is very touchy-feely; we don't need to deal with that when we get into bed later. Water it is!"

"Well, drunk Spencer gets horny-sleepy, and that would be a recipe for disaster."

"We'd end up breaking all our rules." She hesitated, her smile fading, and she grew serious. "Are we sleeping on the sofa bed together? Um, for warmth?" Our eyes locked for a breathless moment, and then she bit her lip and looked away, her cheeks in flames.

"I mean, yeah," I choked out, unable to contemplate not sleeping with her by my side. "The power is out, and it's still pretty cold in here. Plus, the only other option is the holey air mattress upstairs."

"Okay good." Her smile returned as she headed to the sink for water.

"I'll make the drinks tomorrow and take care of the food," I offered. "You've done everything all day. We usually have powdered eggs here. I'll make omelets for breakfast."

She was back to being happy again. "I can't think of a fake food pun for a powdered omelet. Fauxmlet? No, that sucks. Anyway, let's make something special for dinner tomorrow night, maybe spaghetti aglio e olio? We'll have to use jarlic and parm from a canister, but it will still be good because your dad stocked up with some excellent olive oil. It's New Year's Eve, we should celebrate it. I found sparkling cider in the pantry this morning. It's in the fridge in a bowl full of snow. We can toast to the new year."

"I'd like that a lot."

"And since we won't be doing any kissing, we can use all the garlic we want," she teased.

"Perfect."

I watched her move about the kitchen. I could handle this. Last night in bed with her had been hectic, freezing, and frantic. We hadn't had time to think about the implications of being next to each other all night. The intimacy of the situation was moot because we were both too worked up to contemplate it.

But tonight was different. I had all day to think about her, and I was afraid I would get worked up in an entirely different way.

We had been drinking amaretto sours. They tasted sweet, like Christmas cookies, but packed a punch that gave me a pleasant buzz. We had also been snacking on a charcuterie board that Lucy referred to as "cheapcuterie" since it consisted of spray cheese, various crackers, pickles, olives, chicken salad she'd made from a can and a jar of maraschino cherries. All of these were on her top twenty list of favorite foods, she had informed me. I had no complaints; I'd eat anything she put in front of me and be happy about it.

Getting to know her better was like starting a book and knowing within the first couple of chapters that it would become your favorite. And just like a great book, I never wanted this time with her to end.

She returned with our water, and after a few more rolls of the dice, I lost the game, feeling as though I had lost my heart as well.

"Should we sit by the fire? You look sleepy, Spencer."

"I'm getting there. But I want to go wash up first."

"I took a sponge bath while you were out with the wood—it was unsatisfying. I'll make the bed tonight. You go and relax with your sad little pot of hot water."

I let out a chuckle. "Thanks." I got up to heat some water on the stove. "Would you like some water too?"

Yes, please. I always wash my face before going to bed."

"You got it." While watching absentmindedly, I filled a pot and the tea kettle as she cleaned up the Monopoly game.

She sorted the pieces and put them away, and I had

the odd thought that my life was falling into place, just like the parts of the game in the box.

For once, the thought of planning for the future didn't scare me because I wanted her in it. Whatever happened here in the cabin would not be over once we left. I'd make sure of it.

I put the kettle on the countertop. "The water is ready, Lucy. You can go wash your face."

Leaving the now neat and tidy game on the table, she met me at the counter with a smile. "Thanks. I won't take long."

I sucked in a breath as she walked away. Not touching her was becoming more difficult with each hour we spent here.

After she finished, I headed to the bathroom with my water, wishing I could take a long, hot shower instead. I needed to relax. She had me wound so tight that I didn't know what to do or how to act.

My face in the mirror was different, and I *felt* different. I had something to look forward to for the first time in years, and I was all in. But at the same time, I was terrified I would mess everything up.

I quickly opened the drawers and lower cabinets, looking for—shamefully, I was looking for the condoms I had stashed in the back last time I was up here. Half of me knew that Lucy and I getting together was inevitable. The heat between us could not be denied.

The better half knew I shouldn't make a move while we were here, but I wanted to be prepared just in case we lost control.

Unfortunately, there were no condoms to be found. One of my brothers must have used them and not replaced them. I had no idea which one it was, but they'd all hear about it when I got home.

I rushed through my sponge bath, shivering from the cold. Even if there were more than one bed here, it was smarter to share our body heat. The fireplace could only do so much to keep us warm.

The bed was made when I returned to the living room. Seeing her in it sent a surge of heat through my body. Now that I knew what it felt like to have her with me all night, I doubted I could sleep without her. It was probably ridiculous to think such thoughts, but they kept coming no matter what logic I employed to get them to stop.

"Get in." She slid over and patted the spot she had just occupied. "I warmed it up for you."

My body knew what it wanted. I ached to get into that bed, pull her into my arms, and let whatever happened happen. But I couldn't allow that. Especially now that I knew for a fact we didn't have any protection. Plus, we'd both had a couple of drinks as well, so I got into the bed and stayed on my side.

"Do you have a New Year's resolution?" she whispered into the dark.

To finally kiss you.

To make you mine.

To never let you go.

My silence was an unintentional answer.

"You can tell me, Spencer." The covers rustled as she turned to her side. "It's not like birthday wishes. You can say your resolution out loud. You're the one who makes it come true."

"Not this one. Not yet, anyway. What's yours?"

"Maybe mine should be kept secret too. I'll tell you what it is when we get out of here."

"Good idea. We need to be careful tonight."

"Well, it's a good thing I'm not tipsy anymore. Touchy-feely Lucy would have gotten us both into trouble."

"I'm not a touchy-feely man. But I like how it feels when your hands are on me—too much."

"Spencer..." her voice was nothing but air between us.

"Are you okay? Are you cold?"

"I'm okay."

I rolled onto my side to face her. Her hair shone like deep gold in the firelight, and her cheeks were a lovely pink. "You must be warm now; your face is turning red."

"Stop it." Her lips curled into a smile. "You're too sweet. You're making it hard to stay away from you."

"No. It's you. I've never in my entire life wanted a woman like I want you right now, But we can't. I rolled over to my back. "Come here."

I pulled her close, and she rested her head on my chest. My heart thundered beneath her cheek. She slid her hand into mine, and I interlocked our fingers, raising our hands into the firelight. The sight of them wrapped around each other solidified something inside of me, and I knew this wouldn't end when we got out of here.

"How can this feel so right, so fast, Spencer? Is this real?"

"It's real, sweetheart." I turned, dropping a kiss on her forehead. "We should go to sleep before we go too far."

Chapter 11
Spencer

I felt her moving restlessly against me.

She moaned, and it woke me up.

Something wasn't right. I could feel it.

I reached for the lantern next to the couch and flicked it on.

"Lucy?"

A low groan was my only answer. She was pale and trembling. I placed the back of my hand against her forehead. She wasn't feverish, thank god. In fact, she was cool to the touch and sweating.

Her eyes flew open and then quickly shut as if she were in pain. "Oh god. Oh no. What—where am I? Oh! Spencer. I'm going to throw up." She lurched out of bed and ran to the bathroom.

I raced behind her with the lantern just in time to

see her fall to her knees in front of the toilet. It couldn't be food poisoning; we had eaten the same things since we got here. And we hadn't had enough to drink to warrant this kind of reaction.

"What's happening? Lucy?" I set the lantern on the counter and pulled her hair back from her face, holding it as she continued to vomit until nothing remained.

She sat back, leaning against the tub. "I have a headache, a migraine." She let her head drop to her bent knees.

I knelt in front of her. "What can I do? I think we have ibuprofen and maybe some Tylenol."

"Those won't work. My medicine is at home. I have a prescription."

"Do you want to go back to bed? Will sleep help?"

She grabbed the towel hanging off the counter and used it as a pillow while slowly collapsing to her side on the floor. "No, I'm dizzy. I'll just stay right here. I'll be okay. Go back to bed."

"Go back to bed?" I scoffed, wondering what kind of loser she had been with who *would* have gone back to bed. "Like hell I will." I scooped her into my arms and stood. "You'll freeze in here. Let me take care of you." I carried her back to bed and tucked her in. "Tell me what you need, and I'll do it. I'll do anything, okay? I mean it."

Her eyes were glassy and filled with tears that she quickly blinked away.

I rushed to the kitchen, found a big mixing bowl in case she needed to throw up again, filled a glass with water, and returned to the bed. "I brought you a bowl and a glass of water. I wish we had Sprite. My dad always gave us that when we were sick."

"Thank you," she mumbled. "Coke would be better for me. Caffeine sometimes helps."

"What about coffee or tea? I can also find some medicine; we always have the basic stuff here. It wouldn't hurt, right?"

"No. It might help a little."

"Use the bowl if you need to, Lucy. I mean it. You're dizzy, so do not get out of that bed."

"Okay." Her voice was weak. It worried me. One of my brothers used to get headaches like this. A couple of times, my dad had to take him to the emergency room.

My worry for her made me frantic. I rushed around the kitchen, searching the cupboards for anything she may need—anything I could possibly find to make her feel better.

I started the kettle and opened the pantry, where my dad usually kept a stash of over-the-counter remedies. "We have ibuprofen and Tylenol."

"Tylenol," she answered weakly.

I poured some hot water into a pitcher and added some teabags for caffeine. I used the remaining hot water to make a hot compress for her forehead. I brought it to the bed along with the medication. I sat on the edge and helped her up. I shook two pills into her palm, and she swallowed them down with her glass of water.

I didn't like feeling helpless like this. Her pain was out of my control, and I couldn't take it away.

"Lie back." I placed the warm cloth over her eyes. "Try to sleep. I'll bring you tea when you wake up unless you'd rather have it now."

Her bleary eyes met mine. "Why don't I listen to my mother, Spencer? She keeps telling me to carry my pills in my purse. And I swore to her I'd never drive the backroads home in the dark and where did you find me? Where, Spencer? I'm so stupid sometimes, always doing the opposite of what she says—"

My heart lurched in my chest. "Hey, sweetheart, no. You're not stupid; don't talk about yourself like that. You probably always go and get into bed when you feel one coming on, don't you?" I ran the back of my hand down her cheek, telling myself I was checking for fever again. But the truth was I needed the contact to assure myself she would be okay.

"Yeah..."

"And the back roads are perfectly safe to drive. No

one expected this snowstorm. It came out of nowhere. Don't be so hard on yourself. Now, is there anything else that would help you? If the tea and Tylenol don't work?"

Her eyes drifted to mine, and my heart banged against my ribs as I was struck by the wistful sadness I saw in her gaze. "My mom used to wash my hair and rub my head for me. Sometimes, I get so frustrated with her, and then I think of all she does for me and how she always takes care of me. I feel terrible. She'd always tell me to let my head float in the water to relax, and it always helped. We had a huge tub like the one here, and lucky for me, I'm so short. But there's no hot water... I'm going back to sleep. It hurts to be awake."

She handed me the cloth and pulled a pillow over her face. "Thank you, Spencer," she mumbled. "I'm sure the Tylenol will at least take the edge off. And that will make a huge difference."

"You let me know if you need anything. Wake me up. I mean it."

"'kay..."

I watched her until her breathing evened out, and she finally fell asleep again. Then, I climbed into bed next to her. One thing I could do for sure was make sure she stayed warm. I lined myself up along her back, close but not touching.

My dad always used to say that sometimes, just

having someone stay close to you when you were out of sorts could make all the difference in the world.

Chapter 12
Lucy

My eyes fluttered open. The sun glowed through the window, and much to my relief, my migraine had simmered down to a dull ache.

I ran my hands into my hair, pressing my palms against my eyes lightly as I took a slow, deep breath.

I would be okay.

This was not an emergency room level migraine. It should fade away with some more Tylenol, a strong cup of coffee, and maybe more rest. At least, I hoped so.

What had now become a familiar warmth radiated from the space next to me, as if I had been cuddling up to a giant heating pad all night.

Spencer.

My heart swelled when I flashed back to last night and how he'd taken care of me.

"Mornin'," his voice rumbled from his chest, deep and gravely, and his eyes were shadowed beneath as if he hadn't gotten much sleep. "How are you feeling?"

"A little better. The medicine helped. But mostly, it was having you here with me. Thank you."

"Of course. There's nowhere else I'd rather be."

He reached for me, brushing the hair over my shoulder as he studied my face. The light touch of his hand sent a warming shiver through me, and I smiled.

"Yeah, so vomiting is always my favorite way to end a fun evening. I bet you weren't expecting to wake up to that."

For some reason, I didn't feel embarrassed. He'd been so efficient, matter of fact, and caring about everything he'd done for me. Never once had he been disgusted or grossed out about anything that happened, and it meant the world.

My headaches had been part of my life since I was a teenager, and they weren't going away. There weren't a lot of men who could handle it—at least none that I'd ever been with could. Something about him soothed me. He'd been a calming presence when I needed him the most and I would never forget it.

Low laughter rumbled next to me. "If you can joke

around, then I guess I have to believe you're really feeling a bit better."

"There's no more danger of throwing up," I informed him. "I'm down to a normal human headache now."

"That's good. You had me worried."

"I'm sorr—totally not sorry," I joked to cover my constant need to apologize for myself.

"Nice catch. No apologies. Stay put. Close your eyes and rest. I'm still on duty."

"What?"

"You're not up to one hundred percent yet, so I'm taking care of you today. And before you even think of protesting—it's non-negotiable."

"Oh—okay. I could use more sleep." I was not about to argue with him. If he wanted to take care of me, I would let him. "The sun woke me up. What time is it anyway?"

"Late. Almost noon. I'm going to grab you some more Tylenol, then you're going back to sleep."

"Yes, sir." I was going for a humorous tone, but it came out like Marilyn again, soft and breathy.

His eyes heated, and he ran the back of his hand down my cheek before getting up. "Rest." A soft smile traced across his face as he looked down at me, then bent to kiss my forehead softly.

Oh my.

I knew he was an affectionate man because, since we got here, I had noticed him holding it back a lot. I had seen him reach out to touch me and then pull away too many times to count.

He came back with a glass of—was that tea? And the Tylenol bottle.

"This is only cold tea, not iced. But you said caffeine would help, right? I'll make coffee and breakfast when you wake up again."

I sat up in bed and took the glass. "Thank you." I swallowed the two offered pills and finished the tea.

When I returned the glass, our hands touched, and I shivered. "Sleep, sweetheart," his tender, whispered voice had my heart racing. I was falling for him and amazed at how fast it was happening.

But was it fast when I'd known him since we were children?

It didn't matter.

My feelings for him were growing regardless of such things as time, logic, or what anyone would think of me if I came out of this cabin in love with Spencer Cassidy.

Last night, when he said he was not a touchy-feely man, I almost laughed in his face. However, the thought that maybe it was *me* who made him want to be this way astounded me whenever I contemplated it. Physically, we were holding back, but emotionally, where it truly counted, we were moving at a pace so swift that it blew my mind.

After a few minutes of watching him move about the space, adding a log to the fire, water to the kettle on the stove for coffee, and all the little things that would take care of us during our stay, I drifted off to sleep.

This time I woke to the moonlight through the window, smiling when I saw Spencer sitting in the chair across from the sofa bed reading a book.

"How are you feeling?" He said once he noticed I was awake.

"A bit better, thankfully."

"About that—I did something."

"What?" I sat up, looking around. "Is everything okay?"

"Oh yeah, nothing bad." He gestured to the edge of the bed, where a bathing suit was draped across the corner. "I have a few pots of water simmering on the stove. I'm going to run you a bath and wash your hair for you. The swimsuit is new; the tags are still on it. What can I say? Charlotte likes to shop."

"Spencer..."

He held up a hand. "Then you can float, okay? Just like you told me. Stay put for now, though. You should eat first. I'll make some toast."

In the kitchen, he added bread to a pan on the

stove, poured coffee from a thermos, and grabbed the Tylenol before coming back to me.

I smiled, half in shock, thanking him without words as I took them.

I owed him so many tacos—infinity tacos—tacos in numbers too great to count—for the rest of his life.

God, how I really wanted him to be mine.

My mind kept returning to last night. I would never forget a single detail of his face as he cared for me, so gentle, so worried. For the first time in years, hope bloomed in my heart. Real hope, not the kind you fool yourself with. But an actual belief that Spencer and I could be good for each other. My soul swelled with feelings that I thought had long since died.

"Are you still dizzy?" he asked, his face filled with worry. I smiled to put him at ease.

"Not anymore." I sipped coffee as he returned to the kitchen to finish the toast.

"Eat," he said after handing me a plate. I set it in my lap and took a bite. He watched me intently as if trying to discern whether I was truly feeling better or trying to make him think I was so he wouldn't keep fussing over me. "You look better," he concluded, tipping his head to the side. "But I'm still taking care of you tonight. Last night was bad. I was worried sick about you."

"I'll let you take care of me," I began, holding up a hand when he opened his mouth to interrupt.

"But?" He drawled as his lips tipped up in a grin.

"But." I continued with a decisive nod, determined to make him agree. "I'm not used to being taken care of like this except for by my mother. I'm feeling overwhelmed right now—a good overwhelmed, the *best* overwhelmed. I want you to agree right now that you'll let me take care of you whenever you need it. However, I want to do it. Please."

"You've taken care of me already, Lucy. I feel like we've fallen into that pattern naturally, don't you think?"

"Yes, but I appreciate you taking care of me last night more than words can express, so I had to say my intentions out loud."

"I understand," he said, his voice deep, rumbly, and brimming with emotion he was trying to hold back. You intend to take care of me."

"I do."

"Then I should let you know that I have a lot of intentions when it comes to you."

"Like what?" My whispered question danced in the air between us.

"First of all, I intend to take care of you. I want you well again."

His nearness made my head spin. He did not

attempt to hide that he was watching me and liked what he saw. We had an undeniable magnetism, and fighting it was nearly impossible.

I gripped the blanket in my fist to hold myself back. Every instinct I had screamed at me to throw myself into his arms. That this was right, this was necessary. This was everything I'd ever needed. But even though I trusted them, I couldn't follow them. Not yet.

"Finish your toast, sweetheart. Come to the bathroom when you finish. I'll start the bath."

I watched him walk away with a rekindled flame of hope burning into my heart.

Chapter 13
Lucy

Spencer had been so good to me that I couldn't help but wonder if he was even real. Like, perhaps I froze to death in my car, and this was heaven. Or maybe I had lapsed into the best coma ever, destined to dream of Spencer for the rest of my unconscious life.

But the cold bite of the wooden floor against my bare feet told me I was, indeed, awake. When I opened the bathroom door and saw a shirtless Spencer standing there waiting for me, the waft of steamy air was a sure sign that I would remember tonight forever because he looked even better than I remembered.

He stood shirtless. Shadows from the lantern hanging by the door cast a stark contrast between the pronounced muscles of his abs and chest, making him look like he was carved out of granite.

Luckily, I managed not to gasp out loud at the sight.

His massive body filled the doorway while one big hand rested on the frame. The perfect sprinkling of dark hair covered the muscled expanse of his broad chest. My helpless eyes drifted down through the line of black hair running between his abs to disappear beneath the low-slung waistband of his plaid pajama pants.

The thought of getting dizzy again so he would have to catch me was tempting, but I resisted. *That would be wrong, wouldn't it?*

A smirk floated across his lips before setting into a benign smile. He knew I was checking him out. But to be fair, I wasn't trying all that hard to hide it anymore.

"I'll leave you alone to change." His voice was dark as sin. He didn't want to leave. I could tell by the muscle ticking in his jaw and the way his eyes roved over every inch of my body before he switched places with me and backed away. "Yell when you're done."

I nodded in answer, entirely at a loss for words.

My heart rate skyrocketed, and my lingering headache throbbed in my temples from the rush of emotions coursing through my body. I wanted his hands on me. I wanted more of this feeling, more of being cared for by a man who wouldn't push for something sexual in the end. Every other man I dated found my migraines annoying and steered clear of me until I felt better. Or they handed me my meds before running for the door as if my headaches were the ultimate cockblocker.

I studied my face in the mirror before changing into the simple black tank suit.

Who was this woman staring back at me who finally had hope in her heart?

"Ready," I called out and pushed the door open. And I was. I was ready to see where this thing with Spencer could go.

He appeared in the doorway, back under control. "I'm not going to try anything. I swear I just want to help you."

"I know that." Never once had that thought crossed my mind. I would have laughed if he wasn't so earnest.

"Do you need help getting in? Is the dizziness still gone?"

"I got it." Carefully, I stepped into the massive tub. My muscles unclenched and relaxed as I sank into the shimmering water—it was the perfect temperature, which I always thought was *almost* too hot. I could feel it in my bones. It was always a strange sensation whenever I was recovering from a migraine. The pain was never just in my head, and I would always forget how tense my entire body would get.

A deep sigh escaped, along with a few tears of relief.

"Is it too hot?"

I swiped beneath my eyes, hoping he hadn't noticed. "No. It's perfect. You have no idea what you've done for me."

He offered me a washcloth, which I took, dipping it into the water to place across my forehead. Then, I put my toes on the tub's edge and stretched out.

From the corner of my eye, I saw him leaning on one hip against the counter, watching me. I grabbed the side of the tub and let my head float.

"Hunter gets headaches like you do," he remarked. "A few times when we were kids, Dad had to take him to the ER. I'll tell him about the hot bath thing, though he's way too tall to fit like you do."

"Is he the oldest?"

"Yep. Hunter, Deacon, Tucker, Brody, me, and Charlotte."

"Damn, I have four half-sisters. We're close, but I've never shared a house with them. What was that like? Did you have to brawl for time in the bathroom every morning?"

"We had four bathrooms, and yeah, sometimes it was a close call."

"God, I hope Charlotte had her own."

He chuckled. "She did. Dad gave her the room with the attached bath."

"Ha! Good."

"Do you want to stay like this? I can leave if you'd rather relax alone."

"No, stay, please." I turned my head to face him. "Having my mom wash my hair was always one of the silver linings of a headache when I lived at home with her. I'd pay someone to wash my hair every day if I could. But I mean, if this is awkward or whatever, I understand."

"I do not feel awkward," his protest was immediate. "There is nowhere else I'd rather be than right here with you. I mean that, Lucy."

A charged silence filled the air. I saw him grab the shampoo bottle and kneel at the tub's edge, resting one hand near my head.

"You don't give me butterflies," I blurted out.

"Ouch." His face fell into a mask of uncertainty. "You know how to make a guy feel good."

I sat up, accidentally splashing water over the side of the tub in my haste to bring back his smile. "No, this is better than butterflies," I clarified, covering his broad hand with both of mine. "With you, I feel like I'm sinking into a warm bath—just like this one. Or like I'm finally coming home after a long day. You don't scare me, is what

I'm trying to say. I'm not sitting here wondering how this thing with you will fall apart or what you'll end up doing to hurt me. For the first time in my life, I have hope. I trust you, Spencer. I've never felt this way before."

His eyes gentled, growing contemplative. "I trust you too. I want you to know that I'm falling for you, Lucy. I think something inside of me always knew this would happen if I ever had the chance to get close to you."

"I feel the same way. I've always had a thing for you since high school."

His words lit me up inside. Having him confirm out loud what I'd been suspecting he felt was a heady feeling. Having my feelings reciprocated meant I was right to trust my gut when it came to him, which meant more than anything. After so many letdowns, this thing with Spencer was repairing my heart piece by piece.

"I liked you too, Spencer. I was just too shy to do anything about it."

"I don't want this to end when we go home." He did not attempt to be cagey with his feelings, to keep me guessing and uncertain, and it set something free inside me. Each day here had me opening up to the possibility of being with him more and more. Tonight might push me over the edge.

"It won't end, Spencer. I won't let it." I tightened my grip on his hand. I wanted to pull him into the tub with me, but this wasn't the time to let my physical desires eclipse the real and heretofore unprecedented feelings flowing between us. "I'm pretty stubborn," I confessed to lighten the mood. "I've also been told I'm clingy and needy—previously described as negative traits that might work in your favor when we get out of this cabin. We shall see. I mean, you should know what you're getting into if you want to be with me."

"Ah, I get you." Teasing laughter lit up his eyes. "Well, I've been told that I'm too bossy in bed, and I should stop thinking I know what's best all the time. I'm also a know-it-all, and I should never grow a beard." He hadn't shaved since we got here, and his beard was sexy.

I let the bed comment slide because, *yum*. I felt those words right in a spot I shouldn't be thinking about when I was sitting here practically naked in front of him, and he was not wearing a shirt. "Do not shave the beard. Not anytime soon, anyway." Back to joking, "Oh! We can't forget what Skip McFadden said about how I should dress to impress and wear more makeup."

His low, throaty laugh filled the room. "Sweetheart, you're gorgeous. You'll always be gorgeous, no matter what you wear."

My heart fluttered in my chest, threatening to burst through my ribcage and fly around the room. "That's one more reason I'm into you so much. I've looked like hell the entire time we've been here. Clearly, you like me for my sparkling personality and not my looks. I even threw up in front of you, and you seem to like me still. It's a refreshing change of pace. And for the record, I'd still be into you if you shaved your beard. You're gorgeous, with or without it. It's just that I'm curious about—" I flicked my eyes down his unbelievable, carved-out-of-stone bare chest, then back up to let them linger on his mouth—"*Things*. I've never dated a man with a beard before."

"*Things*, huh?" He ran a hand down his beard, and his expression grew dark as he pinned me in place with his eyes. "I look forward to showing you all the *things* then."

"I'm making a mental list."

His lips tipped up at the corner in a sly smile. "Don't forget that I'm bossy and always know best."

"There is literally no chance in hell I'll forget those things, Spencer. Don't you worry about that."

For a brief moment, we sat there, eye to eye, sharing our breath, getting lost in a way we couldn't joke our way out of. There was no way to lighten the feelings that passed between us anymore. He reached out and stroked his hand down the length of my hair, lingering at the ends where it was plastered against my skin before letting the wet strands slide through his fingertips.

"We should wash this before the water cools off." This prolonged anticipation would kill me, and I knew he felt the same way from the look in his eye.

"Mmm-hmm..." With just that slight touch, I felt tingling all over. Words had escaped me.

"How is your headache?"

"It's practically gone. Hot water always does wonders."

"Good. Let's see if I can take it all away. I hated seeing you in pain." He filled his palm with shampoo while I turned my back, anticipating how it would feel to have him touch me again.

Waiting was so stupid. I wanted him right now. Truthfully, I had gone beyond wanting. I needed him.

His big hands tunneled into my hair, rubbing the suds into my scalp with light circles of his fingertips.

My senses reeled as if I had short-circuited. I breathed lightly through my parted lips, trying to regain control over my emotions. I had to respect his boundaries—it was the right thing to do. But my heart wasn't listening; it had swelled with feelings I never knew were possible for me to have. The word "forever" suddenly had a new meaning, and I wanted to start on it now. I was free-falling as everything I had ever hoped for and secretly wished for was coming true around me.

He reached for the showerhead and began rinsing

my hair. He was achingly gentle, careful not to pull or let the shampoo get into my eyes. He had taken such good care of me the entire time we'd been here.

"All right, Lucy." He placed the showerhead on the hook by the faucet. "I'm finished. How do you feel?"

"So much better. Thank you for this, Spencer." Facing him, I watched as he dried his chest with a towel and then pulled his T-shirt over his head.

"I'll leave you to finish up."

He lingered in the doorway. And his eyes were heartrendingly tender. I took it all in, freezing in place to memorize this moment—how his eyes crinkled at the corners, his lips tipped up with his sweet smile, and most of all, how he made me feel like I was the only woman in the world.

I pulled the plug, carefully exited the tub, and wrapped myself in a towel. He'd left the hoodie he was wearing this morning on the counter. Instead of putting on the shirt he'd set out for me, I slipped it over my head and zipped it to the top, before donning the leggings and fluffy socks he had chosen for me to wear.

The hoodie smelled like him. I inhaled deeply and stifled a groan, vowing that I would be wrapped in his arms one day and wouldn't need to sneak into his shirts to feel this close to him. I could get a hit of his scent anytime I wanted.

Chapter 14
Spencer

I had to get out of that bathroom. I was hard as a fucking rock, and I didn't want her to see how much she was affecting me. We agreed not to start something while we were here. I couldn't go back on that, especially since it had been my stupid idea in the first place, and there were no damn condoms available in case we lost control, which was highly likely given how we were getting closer with every passing moment.

Keeping my distance was vital. Being close and touching her became more and more essential with every second I spent with her, and it could not happen tonight. Washing her hair had been too much for me. I palmed my erection, willing it to go away.

I stopped to look outside, where the relentless snow was still falling. I placed a hand on the pane and stared into the dark, leaning my forehead against the glass to cool my racing thoughts. But heat rippled up my spine despite the icy press of the glass against my face.

It was late. The sun had long since set.

We'd slept the morning away together, and then I spent most of the afternoon reading a book while Lucy continued to sleep off her headache.

She'd been so peaceful, so beautiful—I'd never seen a face as pretty as hers. She was lovely, with the twin dark fans of her lashes resting against her delicate cheekbones and the light constellation of freckles sprinkled across her nose. Her face was relaxed, so her dimple was just a tiny shadow on her cheek. I'd wanted to kiss it and wish her good dreams.

I had to grab the book so I didn't spend the day getting lost in my feelings and watching her as she slept.

Each morning here, we'd woken up all over each other. We did in our sleep what we couldn't allow to happen when we were awake.

This was not the direction I should let my thoughts go in. I let out a frustrated growl. I had never been an impulsive man, but something about Lucy made me want to deconstruct my carefully built walls and let myself go.

Needing something to do, I headed to the kitchen

and gathered the ingredients for pasta. I laid out plates, silverware, and glasses on the island.

The water was simmering in the pot when she came out of the bathroom dressed in leggings and the hoodie I'd left on the counter. It was huge on her, and the sight of her wearing something that belonged to me had my stomach turning somersaults and my heart racing out of control.

"I hope it's okay that I'm wearing your hoodie. It looked cozy and warm."

Why was this sexier than that black bathing suit?

I had to look away. Turning back to dinner, I dumped the noodles into the water.

"Yeah," I cleared my throat. "Of course." It was more than okay. It was everything.

She was going to be mine.

But I'd wait until we got out of here to tell her that.

"Pasta for dinner?"

"Yeah, are you hungry?"

"Starved." She slid onto the stool at the island. "Should we wait to have the cider at midnight?"

My lips twitched. "Ahh, yes, let's save the toast for what is arguably one of the most romantic times of the year," I teased.

"The midnight kiss." Her eyelashes fluttered play-fully. "No pressure there." She added with a mock pout, "I didn't get one last year. Unless you count the one on my cheek from my mother."

"I did." I met her eyes over the counter. "And it was not worth the trouble."

Tonight would mark a year of me being alone. No dates, no one-night stands, no flirting, no texting, talking, hoping, or planning—nothing because I had been done with trying.

Cut to finding Lucy on the side of the road...

"Oooh, there's a story there." With her elbows on the counter she rested her chin on her hands. "Tell me all about it."

"It's nothing, really, just the typical not right for each other, wanting different things out of life stuff— which basically sums up the entirety of my dating life. The only story I care about is the one happening right here with you." I touched her nose with a fingertip. "Compared to now, everything else feels like I was just passing the time."

She sat up straight, shaking her head. "How do you do that?"

"Do what? Am I in trouble?" One glance at her playful grin told me I wasn't.

"If I were a Victorian, I would have swooned, Spencer. Like, you'd have to carry me to the fainting couch and put some freaking smelling salts under my nose to wake me up."

"What—?"

Her stunning eyes warmed on mine. "What I love most about you is that this stuff just comes naturally. You're not saying sweet things to get me into bed or placate me somehow. In fact, the only reason why I haven't already jumped your bones is out of respect for you."

"Lucy—" I had to set her straight.

"You're a romantic, Spencer," she cut me off before I could explain. "Any woman who couldn't make it work with you is a complete idiot or dead inside."

"I'm not a romantic—"

"Bullshit." She threw her head back and laughed, sending a cascade of butterscotch waves over her shoulders. I wanted to tangle my hands in it. I wanted to pull her into me and let myself go.

Shit.

"It's you." I blurted.

"What?" Curiosity shone in her eyes. She inhaled a sharp breath, holding it as she waited for my answer.

"In the bathroom, when we were joking around about our relationship flaws, I left something out."

Her eyebrows shot up. "Tell me. I won't judge you. This is a safe space." Her smile was as kind as it was beautiful. I knew right then I could tell her anything.

"I'm not romantic," I confessed. "Not one bit. I've

been called cold. Good at orgasms and bad the romance."

"Noooooo. I don't believe that." She slapped a hand on the countertop. "The hell you say."

"I'd given up. New Year's Eve last year didn't go well. We broke up for petty reasons not even worth mentioning, and that was it. The next day, I went to the shelter down in Sweetbriar and got a dog for company. I don't like living alone, and I was done trying to find someone to be with; it was going to be just him and me. We go for slow jogs every morning; he loves watching football with me, and yeah, he's great."

Her head jerked back on her neck. I'd surprised her. "No shit?"

"None. Zero shit."

"Where is he? Is he okay?"

"Yeah, Tucker—brother number three—picked him up for me. He's hanging at his place with him and his kids until I get back home. He loves kids."

"Okay, good. I was thinking of getting a dog for the same reason—I'm supposed to be on a man-ban, but clearly—" She gestured to me, then back to herself, then around the room with a wave of her hand. "I'm not good at sticking to any sort of rules. Anyway, I also thought about getting a cat but couldn't decide, so I got some fish. I have a big-ass aquarium in my living room."

"That's cool."

One of the things I liked best about Lucy was how we could talk about anything. Jumping from subject to subject, serious or not, without missing a beat.

"It really isn't. Fish are boring as hell. You'd better stir that pasta, Spencer."

"Oh yeah." I turned back to the pot. Luckily, it was not stuck together too badly and was ready to drain. I dumped it in the colander and gave her a smile while I was at it.

"What's your dog's name?"

"Larry. He's a Newfoundland. He might be bigger than you are."

"Hey, just like my Larry the Llama stories!"

"Yeah, I named him after your Larry. Tucker's kids love your books."

I paused, taking in the way her face was lit up, and my heart jerked in my chest. "Damn, Lucy," I whispered through yet another subject change. "I want to kiss you so bad right now. But if I do, I'll never be able to stop."

She leaned forward across the counter. "Why would we have to stop? I understood your reasoning on the first day. You're so sweet. And respectful and protective, and—okay, I'll stop getting sidetracked by listing all your awesome qualities. You didn't want to take advantage of me. But it's different now. You know it wouldn't be taking advantage, right?"

"It's because we don't have any protection here."

"Huh?" Her brows dropped down in confusion.

"Condoms, Lucy. I kept a box in the bathroom cabinet, and they're gone. Believe me, my brothers will hear about it when I get back."

Her eyes widened and she flopped back in her stool as the realization that now we were bound to our agreement and couldn't change our minds hit her.

"Well, damn. Okay. Crap, this changes things. I mean, I wasn't going to try to tempt you on purpose. But I admit, I was halfway hoping you'd change your mind."

"I have to be honest with you. I changed my mind when I went looking for the condoms. Or at least I was more open to seeing where things between us could go. And for the record, I didn't expect sex from you, but I also didn't want to, uh, get something going and not have the option if the need arose."

She huffed out a disgruntled breath. "Maybe I'll join you whenever you have a chat with your brothers. I'm not on the pill or anything. I've been tested and all that, but—how sad for us. We deserve so much pity right now."

"We need one of your silver linings," I said. "We have the pasta? Speaking of—" I added butter, a bit of olive oil, some seasonings, and minced garlic to the pan heating on the stove. "It's the fourth best thing after sex," I informed her as I stirred.

She burst out laughing. "What are the other two?"

"My chocolate chip cookies and—" I shook my head. "Never mind. This isn't the time."

"It's naughty, isn't it? Tell me. Wait, no, don't tell me. I want to guess."

I added the noodles to the pan before turning back around to send her a smirk because I knew it would rile her up. "You'll never guess."

"Wanna bet?" She held up a hand. "I forgot something too. I mean from the bathroom chat about our flaws. I'm—" She used her fingers to air quote. "Too competitive. Whatever."

"Sweetheart," I drawled. "Come on now, I already knew that. The Monopoly game yesterday made it crystal clear, and it's not a deal breaker for me. It's the opposite, if I'm being honest. No worries."

"Opposite?"

"It was sexy as hell. You beat the shit out of me, and I loved it. I don't care what it says about my manhood."

"Oh, well, that's good to know." She bit her lip, and I chuckled as she grew lost in thought. "Okay, I'll put a pin in that to contemplate later."

"Whatever you say." I placed a plate of pasta in

front of her and sprinkled parmesan cheese over the top. "Say when."

After a few beats, she tapped a cute little pink-painted fingertip on the counter. "When, thank you. Come around here and sit by me." I scooped my serving and joined her on the other side of the island. "Let's talk about Spencer Cassidy's hierarchy of needs." She nudged my shoulder with hers. "Number one: Sex. Two: Chocolate chip cookies. Number four is pasta. What could number three be?" She tilted her head to the side, making a show of thinking it over. "I got it: Blow jobs."

I couldn't control my burst of laughter. "Ah, you're so close, but not quite there." It's a good thing I hadn't yet taken a bite, or I would have choked on it.

"Close? Food and sex, food and sex," she murmured. "Ohhh!" She grabbed my arm, shaking it excitedly. "I got it. I bet you're a giver. Everything about you says you'd be generous in bed. Isn't that right, Spencer? You said you were, "*Good at orgasms but bad at the romance.*" That's it. Wow. Okay then." She let go, slugging my shoulder lightly. "You're a downtown man, aren't you?" She didn't wait for an answer before holding her palm up for a high five. "I approve."

I smacked her hand lightly, wondering what it said about me that I was now hard from this ridiculous conversation. No, it wasn't the conversation. It was simply *her*. It was the leggings like a second skin, the fact that she was wearing my hoodie and looking far too sexy in it to be real. She made me laugh. She touched my heart. It was everything about her. All of it.

"Should we really be talking about this right now?" My grin slid sideways as I watched her face flush. "If I recall correctly, we're supposed to stick to non-sexy topics. And yeah, I know I'm equally guilty of breaking the rules."

Her need to win, to guess my number three, outweighed her need to be discreet, and it was hilarious. I almost told her it was actually number two, but I didn't want her to think I was a horndog pervert.

"We're mature adults, right, Spencer?" She sipped her water, the picture of innocence. "What's a little sex talk going to hurt?"

I glanced at her from the corner of my eye. Looking directly at her would only serve to make my dick get harder, like staring straight into an eclipse and going blind.

"We're two mature adults who can't do anything about the raging attraction between them, you mean?"

"Yeah, that," she squeaked out. "We got this, Spencer. We'll be fine."

Fuck it.

I faced her fully. "So if I told you I wanted to wear

you like a necklace, it wouldn't affect you at all, Miss Mature Adult?"

"Uhhh." Her eyes were as big as saucers. She blinked, then blinked again.

"You're driving me fucking crazy, Lucy."

"Oh yeah? Well, I'm not fine anymore." She squirmed in her seat, and I yanked my napkin into my lap to hide my erection. "I mean, seriously, I'm not going to lie to you. I haven't been fine since I got here. You're driving me equally crazy, all right?"

"Let's eat," I suggested, raising my fork like a glass for a toast. "You're right. We're adults, and we want what's best for each other. We got this."

"Oh, right? Cheers to the fourth best thing we could be doing right now." She grinned, rolling her eyes as she stuffed a huge bite into her mouth.

I followed suit, twirling noodles around on my fork.

Then, side by side at the kitchen island, we shoveled pasta into our faces, and I tried not to think about the top two things we would not be doing later tonight.

Shit.

Chapter 15
Lucy

We ate in companionable silence, and I was pleasantly surprised it was only twenty percent awkward. Our repartee since we got here was serving us well. That and the fact that we'd known each other forever helped us bridge the gap between lifelong kind-of, almost, sort-of friends and two people who currently wanted to screw each other senseless.

"We need music," he stated, getting up to grab the radio. "Something to distract us." He stacked our plates and took them to the sink to rinse.

"I totally agree. I don't like quiet. Silence makes me want to fill it, and everything currently running through my mind to say to you is inappropriate for our current situation."

"Damn." He froze in realization. "You don't even

have to be overtly flirty with me, Lucy. In fact, you can try to be the opposite of flirty, and I'll react. Something about you just does it for me."

I shifted my eyes to look at him through my lashes as every feeling I had always wanted to feel and never thought I would shot through my body like a lightning bolt. "I apologize for not being sorry."

He burst out laughing. "Never stop."

My face scrunched up as I realized I wasn't doing anything but being my authentic weirdo self. "Wow. I just realized you make me feel like it's okay just to be me. It's not my fault you have a nerd-kink, Spencer."

"You're fucking irresistible is what you are, and I'm glad you're being yourself around me. I think I might have a Lucy kink. Like I said before, it's you."

Sexy electricity arced through my brain, scrambling it as it shot through my heart and ended up straight between my legs.

"And you're the hottest, most charming, loving, caring, kindest man I've ever met. *You* never stop. How about that?" That electricity also zapped around in my mouth a little bit. So naturally, I started babbling, cringing inwardly as words poured forth without thought—or rather, with too many thoughts happening at once to sort through before I spewed them out.

I was the walking-talking definition of *too much*. I always had been.

"You've brought all that out in me, Lucy. It's all you."

Something clicked into place, and warmth radiated as I allowed his words to sink in.

Maybe I should go outside, shove my head in a snowbank, and cool off. I couldn't be here wearing a lovestruck look on my face like a fool. I had to find a way to be mentally present.

I watched him, trying to think of something to say, as he fiddled with the radio. "There, finally. Got it." He placed it next to me on the island.

The slow beat of one of my mom's favorite songs filled the silence, and I perked up.

"Oh! I love this song."

"What is it?"

"It's "Holding Back the Years" by Simply Red. It's on my mom's eighties playlist." I slid off my barstool and held out my hand. "Dance with me, Spencer. I can't just sit here anymore. I have to do something."

My invitation hung heavy in the air between us for one terrible second.

So I took the few steps to the window and looked outside. The sight of pity on his face would be unbearable. It would crush me. I wasn't quite sure what had prompted me to ask him to dance, but it was too late to take it back now. A nervous knot rose in my throat, but I choked it back.

He inhaled a breath as if to speak, then hesitated, holding it as the silence crashed against me like waves on the beach.

I wanted to cover my ears with my hands or run away; anything other than hearing him say dancing together was a bad idea.

But before I could make a joke about it or laugh it off, he answered me. "Like the dance we didn't get to have together at prom?"

Before I could turn around, I knew he was already there, standing at my back. The warmth of his body eased into mine. My shoulders relaxed as I inhaled a slow breath and turned around.

"Exactly like that. But I'm sure we both have much better moves now."

Explosive currents raced through my body as he stepped toward me, his hand outstretched to take mine. I took it, then pulled him the rest of the way in with my fingers in his belt loop.

I tipped my head back, chin on his chest, hand on his waist. He pressed our intertwined hands next to my cheek, leading us in a slow, swaying side step.

"It's your turn to tell me what you want, Spencer," I whispered. I wanted him to say it out loud. All the things we had in common, the way we wanted to be with each other. I needed him to define it so I could sink into it and believe it. It might be too soon, but I needed a declaration.

"You." His voice, low and sensual, sent a shiver of awareness through me. "I want you, Lucy."

"I want you too," I said on an exhale.

My heartbeat seemed to match the slow pulse of the music as my knees went weak.

He wrapped a big arm around my waist, hauling me against him with a deep, knowing laugh. "I got you, sweetheart."

"But I meant—remember our first night here? When I told you what I wanted."

Light flickered from the fireplace, casting the room in a golden glow while stars lit up the sky outside. This cabin couldn't be more romantic if it tried.

"I remember." He bowed forward, touching his forehead to mine. "Something real," his whispered voice filtered between my ribs, burrowing into my heart as his gaze seared into mine. "This is real, Lucy. You're so fucking beautiful right now."

He pulled back, brushing my hair over my shoulder before stroking my cheekbone with his thumb.

"Tell me more. Please?"

"I want what you want, all of it. I want *real*. I feel it with you."

"I feel it too, with you. I feel *everything* with you, Spencer."

"Good." He paused, studying my face for a beat before a gleam of vulnerability entered his eyes. "We're safe with each other, aren't we?"

"Yes, we are." I snuggled closer into his arms, pressing my cheek against the broad wall of his chest. Sighing when he kissed the top of my head, then letting my eyes drift shut as his chest expanded on an inhale.

One song faded into the next as we held onto each other and let the music carry us away.

"I want to be like my dad," he whispered into my hair. "Honorable, a good husband and, if I'm lucky someday, a father. I don't just want to have a wife and kids, Lucy. I want to create a family. I want to participate in all of it and be a true partner. I want to be with someone who understands me. Someone who sees me for who I really am. But what I want the most is to watch TV in bed on a Saturday night after going to dinner or a walk in the park or whatever."

I pulled away to look at him, and I swear my future flashed in front of me. The two of us here, years later, happy, maybe curled up on the couch watching TV...

His gaze seared into mine, and I saw everything I'd ever wanted right there in his eyes.

"I see you, Spencer." My breath hitched as I tried

not to cry. "I see you so freaking hard. I see nothing but you."

"I see you too. Damn, Lucy. This is torture, but I wouldn't change a thing about it." He buried his face in my neck and breathed in, curling a possessive hand around my hip as he pulled me closer.

All pretenses had faded away. The dance was now only an excuse for us to touch each other. Nothing in this entire world mattered more than me and him and this perfect moment.

"Ten, nine, eight—" A voice from the radio began counting down.

My eyes flew open. "It's almost midnight, Spencer."

"...three, two, one." The sound of fireworks exploding from the radio filled the cabin.

"Happy New Year, Lucy," he whispered hotly into the side of my neck. My hair ruffled from his breath, and I shivered.

I looked up. His eyes darkened with emotion, reflecting everything I felt for him back at me. I knew this was it—he was the one.

My breath caught in my lungs as my lips parted.

Chapter 16
Spencer

*S*he didn't get a kiss last year.

It only took half a second of thought before I ran my hands into her hair and raised her face to mine. I dipped low, brushing my nose along hers, smiling when she let out a sweet little gasp.

My hands shook as I held her tight, clutching her to me, sliding them down the delicate length of her spine, then back up to cup her gorgeous face in my palms again.

"Can I kiss you, Lucy?" We were so close; her lips ghosted against mine as I spoke.

One kiss. What harm could it do?

Not kissing her would hurt her. It would hurt me too. Every second I didn't kiss her was a mistake I was making and determined to rectify.

"Yes. God, yes."

"I've wanted to do this for a long time." My voice was like gravel, low and desperate, as if I'd pulled the words straight out of my soul. "Even before we came here, I've wanted to. Every time I saw you in town, I thought about it."

On her tiptoes, she closed the distance between us, pressing her lips to mine with a sexy little whimper. Her hands on my shoulders wrapped around the back of my neck and into my hair, giving it a light tug to bring my face lower to hers.

"Please..." That word, that sweet little plea for more, lit a fuse in me. I would give her anything. Do anything. Be anything she needed.

Amazingly, I hadn't realized the depth of how much I wanted her until her lips touched mine. My heart exploded. It ached for her. I couldn't deny it now.

It was even harder to deny the hard bulge in my pants now that she was pressed so tight up against it.

Slanting my head, I licked into her mouth and felt a shiver when her tongue slid against mine. Her lips were everything I'd ever imagined. She was soft, sweet, so fucking delicious.

But this kiss would never be enough. I needed everything she had to give.

We traded breath, traded the sounds we made. We breathed each other in until we were full of each other, and nothing else remained but the two of us, this cabin, the snow still swirling outside, and the firelit little world we had discovered together inside these walls.

Breaking the kiss, she pulled away.

Her lips were red, puffy with our kisses, and parted in amazement. I rubbed my thumb against her lower lip, groaning when she darted her tongue out to taste it.

"God, Lucy. I'll never get enough of you." That was all I could think of to say. But it was the truth.

I kissed her forehead and that cute little dimple on her cheek. Then, with my heart bursting for more, I returned to her smiling lips.

"I've spent too much of my life not being kissed like this," she whispered, and I sucked in a breath at her words, silently vowing to kiss her exactly like this every day for the rest of my life. "Tell me this is real, Spencer. Tell me it won't go away when we leave this cabin."

"It won't." I traced a fingertip up the delicate arch of her cheekbone and into the hair at her temple, brushing it back so I could press my lips there. "I won't let it end," I whispered into her ear. "I swear."

We crashed together again, stumbling toward the living room in a tangle of wandering hands, desperate kisses, and the knowledge that we had been correct all along in thinking we would be perfect together.

No woman had ever made me feel this way, overwhelmed, out of control, like my heart was no longer my own.

"I knew it would be like this with you," I groaned against her lips, barely holding myself back from collapsing with her onto the open couch bed.

I took her wrists in my hands, moving them behind her back as I kissed her. "Lucy, baby, we have to stop."

But I was the one who didn't stop. I kept kissing her. As my tongue intertwined with hers, my hands wandered over her body, from her waist to her hips, finally settling on the rounded curve of her ass, squeezing as I pulled her tight against me and ground myself against her.

"I don't want to stop." She pulled away to pant against my mouth. "I want to keep kissing you." She peppered me with little pecks to my neck, chin, and each one of my cheeks, and then she slid her hands beneath my shirt, raising it to kiss the center of my chest. "Let's do whatever we want but keep our clothes on." The shirt dropped back to my waist as she wrapped her arms around me and ran them up my back.

"Oh god. Okay," I conceded, knowing I could never say no to her. But fuck, I might have to.

I walked us backward and sat on the big wing chair beside the fireplace. The couch bed still beckoned me, but thankfully, I had resisted the temptation to toss her on her back and get us both naked.

She sank onto my lap with her knees on either side of my hips. We groaned in unison at the contact. I was so fucking hard for her, and she was so warm and soft, and fuck, I knew I would spend the rest of forever making maps of her gorgeous curves, memorizing her taste, her sounds, and the way she made me feel like I was the only man in the world.

I dragged my lips along her jawline, inhaling her sweet scent as I lost myself in the hazy pleasure of finally having her in my arms.

"Spencer." She sighed. "I don't know how much more I can take. I'm one more kiss away from losing my mind. One more touch, and I'll end up begging you not to stop. Maybe we should go to bed. I mean to sleep." Her eyes were glassy with lust, desperate for more. She needed me.

"Let me make you come. Just you." I pulled the zipper of my stolen hoodie down a few inches, the fabric bunching around my hand as I gripped it, biting back a groan when I realized she wore nothing beneath it. "Can I touch you?"

"I can't let you." With a tremulous exhale, she leaned back and held onto my arms, shaking her head no. "That wouldn't be fair to you. Not when we can't finish—"

"Forget about fair." I all but growled. "Remember our dinner conversation, sweetheart? This is what I want. I need it."

"Are you sure?" Her voice trembled with excitement while every fiber of my being vibrated with anticipation.

"Are *you* sure? Better stop me now if you don't want it before I can't stop myself."

I drew a finger down her chest, between her breasts, stopping on the zipper, waiting for her answer, silently pleading that she'd let me go just a little bit farther than we'd expected.

"Yes, I'm sure," she hissed. "Don't stop. I want you so much."

Her gaze never left me as she took my hand and guided it down, down, down, lowering the zipper until the hoodie was open. Then, slowly, she slipped out of it and let it fall behind her on the floor.

Reclaiming her lips, I crushed her against my chest. "Listen to me," I panted against her mouth. "You have to know this is real. Me and you, Lucy. We are real in this place and every place we go. Right here, right now, and for as long as you want me. Do you understand?"

"I understand." Heartbreaking vulnerability filled her voice. "But what if I never stop wanting you?" She breathed into the air between us.

I drew my head back. I had to see her eyes. "Then you'll have me forever."

Her sweet smile started in her pretty brown eyes before unfurling across the rest of her face. Her cute dimple deepened, the cupid's bow I'd become addicted to kissing grew less pronounced as it disappeared in the radiance of her smile, and the flush over her cheeks made me want to see what else I could say to make her blush.

"God, just fucking look at you." I traced a circle around the tip of one of her nipples. Smiling when she arched into my hand in a silent request for more. "You're gorgeous, Lucy, with your sweet, blushing face and these pretty pink nipples. You're like a sunset, a rose. It almost hurts to look at you. You're so beautiful."

"Spencer..." Her eyes glazed over with pleasure before drifting shut.

I leaned forward and drew the hard little tip of her nipple into my mouth with a soft, sucking kiss, smiling against her skin at her soft gasp and gripping her waist to keep her steady as she arched backward.

She leaned forward, hands finding my waist, tugging at my shirt. "Take this off. I want to feel you, too."

Reaching behind my neck, I tugged and yanked the shirt over my head, then blindly tossed it aside.

We lost ourselves in each other again, skin against skin, her breasts flattening against my chest as we kissed each other senseless.

"I've dreamed of this." I broke away from her mouth long enough to whisper. "So many times."

"This is better than a dream." She was stunning—puffy lips, heaving chest, hair a mess from my hands...

She ground herself against me, riding the hard ridge of my cock through our clothes until we were both crazed, and I was thrusting up into all that soft warmth between her thighs as she pushed herself down hard against me.

"These leggings need to go." I breathed into her ear, my teeth lightly nipping her lobe. "I need more of your skin."

We couldn't go all the way, but we could go farther than this.

She scrambled off my lap and shoved them down her legs, kicking them to the side to leave her standing in front of me in a pair of white cotton bikini briefs.

How she made something so simple be the sexiest thing I'd seen in my life, I'd never know.

"These are new," she explained. I'll have to replace a huge Costco pack of undies in that dresser." A chuckle escaped my lips as she twisted her toe on the floor, her face turning from a light blush to crimson.

She was so fucking cute. "Um, you too. Pants off, Spencer."

Lifting my ass from the chair, I slid out of my pajama pants, thankful I'd put on a pair of boxer briefs.

I laughed darkly. "Get back over here."

I reached for her, feeling the smooth skin of her legs as I slid my hands up and gripped the sides of her panties, using the fabric to pull her close and then back onto my lap.

"Let's make each other come," she murmured, sinking down again, pressing her soft inner thighs tight to the outside of mine. "I don't want it without you."

My forehead dropped to her shoulder. Everything faded away but her and how she felt spread across my lap. The way I wished I could feel every inch of her bare skin on mine and how I would die to be inside of her right now.

I trailed the tip of my nose up the side of her neck before groaning into her ear, "Anything you say. Whatever you want." My own needs were the furthest thing from my mind. All I cared about was making her feel good.

She increased her pace. "Is this okay?"

"Fuck yes, it is." I grabbed her hips, clutching her tight, sinking my fingertips into her supple curves as she ground herself hard against my cock. "Anything you do to me is okay, just don't stop. I'm so close."

She didn't answer. Her eyes were wide on mine, lips parted, hips rocking, hands clutching my shoulders as she rode my lap.

"Hurry. Faster, baby. Are you going to come for me, sweetheart? I can feel how wet you are through our clothes, you're so fucking hot." I twisted the sides of her panties, pulling them tight so they would rub against her clit as she moved against me. "Do you know how bad I want to be inside of you right now? You're going to take me so well, Lucy. It's going to feel like heaven on earth when we're finally together, when I can fuck you like you need me to."

"Spencer, oh my god—" Her breath hitched, and her thighs seized as she ground herself against me, sending us both over the edge.

I kissed her again. Wet, messy, perfect. Then I picked her up, legs around my waist, and took her to bed.

"All your kisses are mine now, Lucy. Do you hear me? Midnight or not. New Year's Eve or not—all of them. We're falling in love with each other right here in this cabin."

She didn't speak. Her head nodded against my chest as she sighed.

"I'll be right back." I kissed her cheek and then got up. "You made a mess of me, sweetheart. I have to change."

I didn't care that this thing with her happened so quickly and unexpectedly. Lucy was now an essential part of my life. This was right. This was real. We were perfect. And we did not need to define it or explain it to anyone.

Chapter 17
Lucy

He was back; I sighed as he scooted in behind me, yanked me against his body, and wrapped me up tight in his arms.

It hadn't even been a week, but he was wrong, I wasn't *falling* for him. I had already fallen. I was ninety-nine percent sure that I was in love with Spencer Cassidy.

I'd be coming out of this cabin floating on a freaking cloud. I could probably fly back to my house right now if I wanted to. Who needed a snow plow and a rescue attempt to get home? Not this girl.

I snuggled under the covers and deeper into his arms with a sigh. He was always so warm, and I would never get enough of him.

The only thing that eased my mind about the quickness with which I had fallen for him was that I'd known him since kindergarten. So maybe this was just a life-long slow burn instead of a desperate attempt to avoid being alone. My feelings were real. We made too much sense together for this to be a lonely delusion.

I still had found no words to say to him. All I could hear was his words echoing in my head.

"Do you know how bad I want to be inside of you right now? You're going to take me so well, Lucy. It's going to feel like heaven on earth."

This man had made me come harder *without* fucking me than any man I'd ever been with in my life, and honestly, it was ridiculous. It was also amazing and infuriating.

I could have had *this* all along. Not just the amazing orgasm. But all the feelings that went along with it. His care, protection, and incredible respect for me and our situation were the most important parts.

"I can hear the wheels turning in your head, Lucy. Please tell me that you're okay?"

I froze in his arms, thinking how much to tell him before deciding to spill my guts. I'd been doing that the entire time we'd been here, and it didn't seem to bother him, so why not continue being an open book?

"Yeah. I mean, no. We could have been fucking each other stupid and making each other happy for years, Spencer. We both liked each other. We were both interested. I'm a little bit disgruntled about that fact right now."

The bed shook as he burst into laughter behind me. "God, you make me laugh."

I spun to face him. "It's not funny."

"You're right. It isn't." His hands drove into my hair as he pulled my face to his and kissed me before continuing. "But who knows if it would have worked between us before? Maybe we're meant to be together now when we're both ready for it?"

I contemplated his words. "You have a valid point. I'm definitely ready to be in a happy, healthy relationship."

"Exactly, me too. Maybe we had to suffer through all our bad relationships to know what we *don't* want. And to learn how to treat another person. Which makes this time together all the sweeter, right?"

I settled into his side, sighing when he pulled me close. "Yeah, another good point. You just got me off so spectacularly I couldn't think straight."

A mischievous spark ignited in his eyes. "You were the one doing all the work, sweetheart." His voice was nothing but a husky whisper that sent a thrill through my veins.

"Well, you provided the hard-on." I planted my face in his neck and covered him with kisses. "I wouldn't have had anything to work with without it."

"Good point, Team Snowbound, right?" he conceded, kissing the top of my head.

Instead of our Team Snowbound high five, I kissed the hell out of him.

He pulled back, brushing a hand down my cheek. "How are you feeling? Okay?"

"Yes, I haven't been this happy in ages, Spencer. Thank you."

"I should be thanking you. I have hope again because of you."

I tipped my head back, hoping he would kiss me, then smiling against his lips when he did.

"Sleep, sweetheart." He kissed my dimple and then darted his tongue out to taste it. "This might be my favorite part of your face," he murmured. "But then I'll get lost in your pretty brown eyes or kiss your gorgeous lips and have to question myself."

"See?" I dropped my forehead to his chest, along with another kiss. "Don't ever tell me you're not romantic. When I get home, I'm going to write down every sweet thing you've said to me in my journal so I'll always remember how you made me feel."

"Don't worry, baby, if you forget anything, I'll tell you more."

"You're doing it again, and I love it. I'm so glad you found me."

"Me too. Happy New Year, Lucy."

I inhaled a sharp breath. "Happy New Year."

I wasn't used to feeling like this. I was happy, hopeful, and looking forward to seeing what the future would bring.

Spencer was a gentleman, but he was more than that. He had an innate knowledge of how to take care of someone. He was dependable and steady, and I knew he would be reliable and trustworthy, too. He was every good thing a man should be.

He made me feel safe and turned what could have been an awful circumstance into the beginning of something extraordinary.

I drifted off to sleep in his arms, hoping that all my New Year's Eve kisses would be Spencer's from now on.

Chapter 18
Spencer

I awoke to banging on the window. Squinting my tired eyes into the glare of the sun, I could tell it was late, probably early evening. Lucy and I had accidentally slept the day away. I opened my eyes to see my dad grinning at me as he tapped on the glass. He smiled hugely, gestured to Lucy, and gave me a thumbs-up.

Shit. He had known I was interested in her back in high school when I wanted to take her to prom. I had no idea what he knew about my feelings for her now. He was observant. I was pretty sure he had a running mental file of information on each of his kids. I tried to keep my feelings to myself most of the time, but not that hard. He probably knew I still had a thing for her.

"Wake up, you two! Get dressed before your brothers show up. I could see his truck parked behind him on the trail and a huge trench with snow piled high on each side. He'd obviously just finished plowing his way up here.

"Lucy, baby, wake up." I wrapped her tight in my arms and tugged the blankets higher so she wouldn't sit up and accidentally flash my dad.

We were both still shirtless, but thankfully, she was spread out across my chest again, and what wasn't covered by the blankets was draped in the soft fall of her butterscotch waves.

"Spencer? What's happening? What's going on?" Her mouth fell open in a huge yawn. "Is it morning?"

"Yeah, sweetheart, and my dad is outside. My brothers are on the way."

Her eyes flew open in alarm, and I pulled her close to keep her from flying out of bed. "Crap, Spencer. My boobs are out."

"No one can see—yet. Stay still." My eyes darted to the window. My dad had turned his back so we could get dressed.

Lucy was right before. We needed some curtains for this damn place. At least he hadn't come barging in. That would have been awkward.

I locked eyes with her as thoughts crashed through my brain, whirling and skidding around until only one remained.

I didn't want to leave.

She was warm and so soft; she smelled like heaven, but the bottom line is that she belonged with me. I couldn't see any other way to live the rest of my life unless she was in it.

What was I supposed to do?

What was so certain at midnight felt different in the light of day. Had we gone too far?

I couldn't exactly propose marriage or ask her to move in with me when we'd spent less than a week together. She would think I was out of my mind, and maybe I was—out of my mind for *her*. Being with her was all I could think about.

"I guess we'd better get up," she whispered without moving.

Then she got closer, sliding off my chest to her side, tangling her legs with mine, and burying her face in the side of my neck. She shuddered against me as she drew in a slow breath.

"Yeah." Cradling her head in my hands, I kissed her temple. "I'll get up first and bring you your clothes."

"Thanks." She took a deep breath and forced a smile on her face.

My heart was too big for my chest. It hurt to look at her. Not like last night when I was overwhelmed with anticipation and hope—this time, it hurt like I was losing her, which made no sense. I wasn't losing her, *was I?*

I rubbed a circle over my sternum as I carefully slipped from beneath the covers and stood. The chill in the air matched the cold dread that filtered through my system at the thought of being away from her.

She watched me, eyes luminous and sad, shining in the sunlight filtering through the window.

The fire had died down as we slept, but I guess that was good since we'd be leaving soon.

I found her leggings and my hoodie on the floor and brought them to her. Each item I picked up was a reminder of how we'd stripped each other bare last night, and not just physically. I felt like we had an honest and true connection, and I couldn't wrap my brain around how to proceed from here.

After a glance out the window, she wrapped herself in a blanket and darted to the bathroom with her clothes.

I found the jeans I'd worn the day I arrived folded neatly on one of the chairs at the table. I slipped them on, along with my T-shirt from last night, before sitting down hard and dragging a hand over my beard.

"Are you decent?" My dad shouted.

"Yeah. Come on in."

He came through the door, heavy winter boots clomping across the hardwood and wearing his observant "dad" face as he headed in my direction and took my measure.

"You look like shit." He pulled out a chair and sat. "What's eating you? Did you fall in love with her? You always liked her. You know, back when you were a kid, right after your mom died, you told me you were going to marry her when you grew up. Do you remember that? She's a sweet girl, that Lucy. Your mom liked her."

My head snapped up. "Yeah, she is. She's amazing. I don't remember saying that though. Kinda wish I did."

I could see myself saying it. She'd always been special to me.

"It was a hard time, Spence. I won't say anything to her or your brothers, okay?" His eyes were steady on mine.

"Thanks. Uh—"

He patted my hand, and I knew I'd be okay. "Took us forever to get up here. It's nearly dinner time." His eyes were shrewd on mine. "You slept all day. You two have a late night?"

He was prodding without being pushy. He was good at making observations that would open up an entire conversation. But I couldn't answer him when Lucy and I were still new, and there was so much still left up in the air between us.

"No, um, we, I mean it was New Year's Eve so..."

With perfect timing, my oldest brother, Hunter, popped his head through the door. "Hey," he greeted me. "Brody is driving your truck to the shop. We got it up and running. Deacon has Lucy's car on the flatbed, it was a bitch to dig it out, but we got it. Later, Spence. Say hi to Lucy for me." He added with a teasing smirk.

"Thanks." He wasn't being a dick. He and I could have an entire conversation without uttering a sound. He was curious and would be happy for me if I ended up with Lucy.

"Ignore him. Your brothers have been taking bets about what went on while you were here—"

Immediately, I went from being thankful to pissed. "What the hell? Bets? I won't stand for any shit talk or gossip about Lucy—"

He placed a hand on my arm. "Hold your horses. They know about your thing for her. We all do, Spencer. They're not spreading shit around town or being disrespectful; you know better than that. It was all in good fun and nothing inappropriate. You know I don't allow that kind of shit. Come on now."

Feeling sheepish and also like I'd just laid all my cards on the table. I backed off. "I overreacted. I'm sorry."

His eyebrows shot up as he tilted his head to watch

me. "That reaction was telling, though. Protective." He smiled approvingly.

"Was it?" I hedged. "I don't know what I'm feeling. I mean, okay, I do, but I don't know what to do about it."

His eyes darted toward the bathroom. The water was running, so she must have been washing her face or brushing her teeth. Something was making her take forever, which was good. I needed a minute to gather my thoughts and hear what my father had to say.

"Get her number, son." He tapped the table decisively. "Ask her out."

"That sounds so simple. Ask her on a date." I huffed a laugh. "But how can I do that when everything that happened here is the opposite of simple? We have real feelings for each other, way more than first date stuff."

"Easy. When you leave, you'll be starting over. Just not at the beginning, you get me?" He sat back, crossing his arms over his chest with a satisfied smirk.

"How does that make no sense and describe exactly what this feels like all at the same time?"

His lips tipped up in a wry smile. "It's kind of like life, isn't it? It's impossible to figure out, and you're always starting over because of some bullshit or another. It's frustrating if you think about it too much."

"Hell yeah, it is. Frustrating is definitely the right

word. How is everything in town? I should have asked about that first. Is Larry okay?"

"Everything is fine now. Same old, same old. Hunker down and then clean it all up. Nothing out of the ordinary other than the number of trees that fell up here. They're cleared away now. Larry is fine; you'll have a hell of a time getting him away from Tucker's kids, though."

I shook my head with a chuckle. "Tuck can get his own dog for the kids."

"I was mostly joking. They know Larry is your baby."

The water shut off in the bathroom, and my eyes fell closed as I tried to come to grips with everything that had happened between Lucy and me.

"Hey, you know what to do, okay?" He patted my arm before sliding his chair out from the table. "I'll go wait in the truck. Get your girl."

"Thanks, Dad."

He flicked two fingers out in a wave. "Always."

I watched him walk out, greeting Lucy on his way out the door.

"Where is he going?" she asked.

An odd sense of formality hovered in the air between us—an uncertainty I did not like. I wanted to kiss her, slide my hands into her hair, and make all this doubt disappear. *But should I?*

"He's going to wait in the truck."

"Oh, alright." She stood next to the chair we had used last night—an odd symbol of how far we'd gone while staying in the same place. Would what we found together work in the real world? "I know we said this wouldn't end but, Spencer, I don't know what to say—"

She had changed into the clothes she wore when we got here.

Seeing her dressed like that made this moment feel bizarre and full-circle, as if we'd lived a lifetime in a few days.

Just like my dad said, we had to start over.

She blushed softly as her hands drifted across the back of the chair.

"We need a plan," I blurted. "I have to have a guarantee that I'm going to see you again."

Her whole body seemed to sigh with relief, and she let out a little laugh as she crossed the room and settled into the chair across from mine at the table. I smiled, knowing she wanted to discuss when we would next see each other as much as I did.

She reached for my hand and I took it, raising it to my lips to kiss the back.

"Maybe we can meet in town for dinner—?" Her gaze was direct. She was earnest and forthright and so fucking beautiful.

How had I kept her at arm's length all these years?

Why was I ready now and not then? Timing and opportunity had forced my hand and it was the best thing that had ever happened to me.

I didn't have to say a word, and my dad had read me like a damn book. He knew what happened here.

My heart raced; I didn't want to mess this up.

Whatever part of my heart that had always been hers burst apart, filling the rest with clarity. We belonged together. This was right.

A restless need built in my system, pricking beneath my skin until I was laser-focused on one thing.

Grabbing her chair, I pulled it close, then cupped her chin to kiss her. Her lips were warm and sweet, but now there was an intimacy there. Our chemistry had shifted, and I would not let it shift back. I was determined to keep her in my life.

"I need your number." I whispered against her lips.

"But I—"

I cut her off, pulling away only enough to see her eyes. "A date, Lucy. Friday. Six o'clock. All you have to do is answer the door when I knock and let me take care of you."

"That's it? Just answer the door?" Her lips twitched, and I kissed her. "I can do that. I'll let you in on a little secret, Spencer. Almost every woman dreams of being swept off her feet from time to time."

I wanted to kiss her again and never stop.

I wished we could get back into that chair and finish what we'd started last night, but I held myself back. This woman deserved the world, and I would be the man who gave it to her.

"Good girl." A grin slid across my face as her lush lower lip slid between her teeth. "No driving down the mountain. No meeting for tacos. Just me showing you how you deserve to be treated. I'll take care of everything. Now, what's your number?"

She stilled for a moment with her eyes on mine, hot and full of promises. "I was going to say—you can absolutely have my number, Spencer—I need something to write it down on. Is your phone dead? Mine is, and I haven't seen any paper around here. Or a pen—"

"I won't forget your number, sweetheart. When I want something, I remember it."

Her head dropped, and she rested her forehead on my chin. "So you're not only romantic but hot as hell, too?" She looked up, smiling at me as she gave me her number. "How did I get so lucky?"

"I'm the lucky one in this scenario, Lucy."

"I don't know how I feel about leaving this place. Why can't we stay here? I know it's silly, but I—"

"Shh, I know." I pulled her into my lap and hugged her tightly, burying my face in that sweet spot where her neck met her shoulder so I could breathe her in. I needed another hit. "We'll be okay. I'll call you tonight before bed, I promise."

She was uncertain, and I couldn't blame her. This thing between us had come on fast, and it scared me a little bit too.

I sighed into her hair, ruffling the waves. My chest felt heavy with a strange combination of expectation and worry. Like I was on the precipice of something big and had to let it go to keep her close.

Chapter 19
Lucy

My empty house had never bothered me before this moment. Being alone was something I enjoyed, even preferred. Not anymore, apparently.

Spencer and his dad had barely dropped me off a half hour ago, and I was already moping around like my life was ending without him.

I lived in a cozy log cabin behind the Honeybrook Inn. Much like Spencer's family cabin, I was in the forest. The difference was that mine was not in the boonies. I was only a hop, skip, and a jump away from the Inn and town and takeout coffee.

I had one bedroom, a bathroom, a kitchen, and a living room. Basically, I lived in a girly little square with a wraparound porch. Think pastels, fluffy overstuffed furniture, homemade quilts and knitted throws, my needlepoint, and books everywhere.

It was a rustic log cabin on the outside with old lady décor on the inside. Picturing Spencer in here gave me a thrill. What would it look like to have him naked in my white iron four-poster bed? I almost started drooling at the thought of his chest hair getting caught up in my lacy pink duvet cover. And those big, rough, work-calloused hands of his...

Damn.

I missed him.

I wanted to finish what we started together in that big chair at the cabin.

I didn't want to be without him—maybe ever.

Last night, he told me all my kisses were his. My dating history taught me to take whatever a man says when I am bouncing around on his lap with a grain of salt, but Spencer was different. I believed him.

We had only been stuck in that cabin for a few days, so I knew I was being silly, overly romantic, dramatic, and full of wishful thinking. But I couldn't find it in myself to care because our time there felt real. It was the most I'd been *myself* with another person in a long time, if ever.

We had a date planned, but I was so *bad* at dating that I was bound to screw something up. Back in the cabin, I had quit thinking about how to act and just let myself be myself. We had no choice but to let all of our usual pretenses go in order to stay sane and survive together.

I paced around my kitchen island with my thoughts racing out of control.

The quiet in my cabin pounded in my ears.

My heart constricted, and it felt like the air had somehow thinned. I couldn't breathe.

The reality of the real world outside of our snowy little bubble was slapping me in the face hard, and I didn't like it one bit.

I stopped at the sink and filled a glass with water, gulping it down in a few sips.

Sure, I had electricity and hot water now, but what did it matter if he wasn't here with me?

Like an irrational fool, I darted around my house and flipped all the lights off. I built a fire and threw myself on the couch to watch it crackle and blaze as I got lost in the memories of the last few days.

I was warm, and I had all my stuff, and my fish, and my books, and TV, but I wanted to go cuddle in the dark with Spencer, damn it. I didn't need all these distractions when I was with him.

I'd gone from my Man Ban to the All Spencer All the Time Plan as if I hadn't spent my entire dating life getting my heart broken by mediocre men. My outlook had changed like the crack of a whip, shocking and sudden, like an awakening. I was all in with him. Now, I knew my other relationships had never worked out because I was always meant to be with Spencer. We were perfect together.

Where had my sense of self-preservation gone?

Like a dewy-eyed ingenue, I'd left it somewhere at the Cassidy family cabin. But damn, hopefully, I wouldn't need it anymore.

I didn't even have his number to call him. Our phones had died, and there was nowhere to write his number down. I hoped that he remembered mine because I was missing him like crazy, and I needed to hear his voice. Maybe it was a good thing I couldn't call him since I was halfway to losing my mind over him.

Quit being pathetic.

I should shower, make something to eat, or do anything else but sit on my couch like this sad shell of a woman.

I picked up my mug from the coffee table and sipped it.

Yeah, I had coffee, but it wasn't *his* coffee. I slid it back onto my coffee table with a dramatic sigh. I was ruined for life and spoiled completely rotten because of how well he'd treated me. No other man would do.

My phone charging on the end table pinged with a message. I lurched, heaving myself up to grab it.

Alas, it was not Spencer.

Every one of my half-sisters, my mother and grand-mother, had started texting me. After the first ping, the notifications went out of control. I muted them and sank back into the couch, throwing an arm across my forehead. I knew Spencer's dad had informed them they'd be picking us up today, so they knew I was alive and home. I didn't have to answer yet.

Five minutes later, the knocking started.

I should have gone straight to the shower, damn it. Now, I would have to entertain.

"Come in," I bellowed. I was not getting up to open the door. I was in the mood to mope, ruminate, and pout. Making plans and healthy changes would happen tomorrow. I knew myself; I had to wallow first.

I slid into the corner of my couch and snuggled beneath my knitted throw blanket. I was tempted to pull it over my head and hide, but they'd for sure spot the Lucy-shaped lump beneath it. There was no avoiding the million questions I was not ready to answer. But the silver lining was I'd get it over with at once, even if I didn't know the answers to all of them.

My mother entered the heavy oak door, followed by my half-sisters. Piper and Paige were first. They were from my father's first wife, who he'd cheated on with my mom. Cara was next—she was my age. We were in the same grade throughout school, sometimes even in the same class. We were born a couple of months apart; fun, right? My dad had cheated on my mom with hers when they were both pregnant, but she forgave him and kept him around until he cheated again with Eliza's mom. She was the youngest. Dad left my mom for hers, and they were still married. They moved down to Portland to escape the scandal of having the five of us girls all living in the same small town.

The best and weirdest part of my bizarre family history was that, aside from Eliza's mother, the other moms were now the best of friends, and the five of us girls were all as close as possible. However, it hadn't started that way. It took years of working through bitterness and bad feelings before my grandparents' desire to have us all part of their fold, mothers included, successfully smoothed the rough edges of my father's betrayal and brought us all together as one big, weird-ass family.

Dad's parents owned the Honeybrook Inn, where we spent a lot of time and grew up close. I would never know how my father ended up such a philanderer. None of my aunts or uncles were like him. My grandparents were wonderful, but my father was a constant source of disappointment for them. They loved him but did not approve of his choices at all.

"Are you okay? I was worried sick." Mom rushed to join me on the couch and pulled me into her arms before pushing me back to study my face. "You seem okay." She placed the back of her hand on my forehead, tilting her head side to side as she watched me. "I stopped by and fed your fish."

"We brought food." With arms full of bags and covered dishes, Piper and Paige headed straight to the kitchen.

"Thank you!" I shouted to their retreating backs. "Mom, I have the auto-feeder." I glanced at the tank. The little weirdos were swimming laps around their Sponge Bob pineapple house as happy as could be. "They're okay."

"Well, I couldn't leave my grandfish all by their lonesome and not check to see how they were doing, right?"

"Right, you're too much. They probably like you more than me." I laughed. "Thank you. You're being awfully chill about this whole thing. It isn't like you."

"I've been getting regular updates from Spencer's dad. He assured me the cabin was perfectly safe and fully stocked with firewood and food. Plus, I've known Spencer since he was a little boy. I knew you'd be okay with him."

"That makes sense." I tilted my head, thinking

about Spencer, prom, and her strict rules that prevented her potential early debut as a grandmother of human children instead of my fish babies, but I decided against raising that subject. It was moot, and I was not in the mood to open that can of worms.

Piper sat across from me on the oversized recliner that I liked to read in. "She's fine. The fish are fine. Let's talk about how she's been alone with Spencer Cassidy for the last few days. How about that?"

"How about not," I shot back. "I'm totally fine, Mom. You were right." My attempt at dodging the Spencer topic was weak. Everyone laughed as they found seats around the room.

"Yeah, I bet you're fine," Eliza muttered. "I'd be fine too if I'd been stuck alone up there with a Cassidy man."

"I'd even take their dad," Piper added. "He's like a hot, ripped Santa Claus."

"You'd be his ho, ho, ho, am I right?" Paige nudged her shoulder.

"Damn straight. I don't care how much older than me he is. That man is fine."

"You girls. Stop." My mother scoffed at their objectivation of Spencer's extremely good-looking father. I mean, he got his looks from his dad. There was no doubt about it.

"On second thought, maybe *you* should go for it," Paige told my mother, then watched to gauge my reaction.

"No!" I did not disappoint her with my immediate rejection of the idea.

"And there it is," she boasted. "You don't want your future father-in-law to become your stepfather. Boom!" She raised her hand for a high five.

Piper smacked it, shaking her head and mouthing "Sorry" to me. Paige liked to know everything and was not shy about gathering information in any way she could.

"Yeah, so I might have a little bit of a thing for him." I shrugged, wishing they'd drop it.

Cara, perched on the arm of the couch next to me, put a hand on my shoulder as a silent show of support. She was the only one who knew how deep my crush on Spencer had gone back in high school. She was probably dying to know what happened. But knew me well enough to know I'd tell her everything once we were alone.

"So, did he take good care of you, honey?" Mom asked, pointedly ignoring the teasing.

Paige let out a snort, and I glared at her. "Hey." I stuck my tongue out. "He was a perfect gentleman. I got a migraine the second day, and yes, he took great care of me."

My mother was pleased. "I knew it. I bet you didn't have your medicine, did you?"

"No." My eyes darted to the floor like I was in trouble. Old habits die hard, I guess. "But I was fine. It wasn't a bad one."

"I'm glad. Where's your purse? I'll put a few of your pills in there. Just in case—" She stood and headed toward my bathroom.

"Just in case she gets trapped in a cabin in a random freak snowstorm again?" Piper teased gently.

Mom laughed and headed for the front door instead, stopping with her hand on the knob. "Okay, point taken. I'll back off. But you never know what can happen. That's the point. I always say that forewarned is forearmed. Be prepared. Girls, let's get out of Lucy's hair so she can relax. Decompression is key, honey. Why don't you take a bubble bath? I put some new lavender bath salts on the edge of your tub."

My eyes widened. Was she leaving *without* knowing everything there was to know? She was never one *not* to meddle. My eyebrows dropped down in a low V of suspicion.

Cara kissed my cheek, whispering for me to call her later.

"Grandma sends her love," Piper informed me. "She said she wouldn't add to the nosy inquisition and will talk to you later once you've settled back in. So expect to deliver a full rendition of your snowed-in experience to her at some point in the future."

I huffed a laugh. "Thanks for the warning."

"You got it. Call me if you need anything."

Paige bent to hug me goodbye. "I was only teasing you. If you hooked up with Spencer, I would be very happy for you. He's a good guy."

"Thanks, Paige."

She laughed. "So you're still not going to confirm or deny? Damn, Lucy. Harsh."

Seeing the humor in her eyes, I smiled. "You guys will be the first to know if something happens, okay?"

"Okay. Get some rest. Talk soon."

I watched them leave, then let out a relieved sigh. I wasn't ready to talk about Spencer until I—I had no idea when I would be ready.

With every other relationship I had, I was always talking about it. I was the one who made the effort. I made the plans, thought about my feelings, and wondered how he felt because he never wanted to talk to me about it. I constantly worried about where things were going, while in reality, nothing ever went anywhere, probably because I pushed too hard. I held on too tight, twisting my hope into knots and then crying about it when they unraveled, and I was left alone again.

No more.

I got up to open a bottle of wine and grab a snack. I still had things to ponder.

Spencer said he wanted to make plans. He said all I had to do was open the door for him when he knocked.

Maybe I should let him.

Obviously, the door he was talking about was literal, but maybe there was also a symbolic one. Maybe letting him take the lead would be good for my heart. He had already healed something inside me by giving me room to be my authentic self and not running off into the storm to escape my "too much" qualities.

I opened the fridge and found one of Piper's famous cheese boards. God bless Paige and Piper and their need to feed anyone who was going through some shit.

With a smile on my face, I took my wine and the food and headed into my living room to rot on the couch. I flicked on the TV and tried to find something to watch.

I flicked it off, grabbed my book from the coffee table, and immediately tossed it aside. I was not in the mood to read.

I was in the mood for Spencer.

But I didn't have his number or my car. I could call any of my sisters for a ride, but that would mean admitting things I wasn't ready for anyone to know yet.

Damn.

I hoped lavender bath salts really were relaxing because I was about to dump half that freaking bag into the tub and try to soak out my feelings.

Chapter 20
Spencer

Most Honeybrook Hollow locals chose the Twilight Trails Tavern to unwind over beers and burgers in the evenings. A few times a week, I'd meet one or more of my brothers there to play pool and relax.

Although this place was a dive, it was warm and comfortable. It was all dark wood and burgundy leather booths. A big, roaring fireplace flanked by deep green couches was in one corner. In another, a couple of pool tables surrounded by high-top tables were visible through an arched entrance. Old country western music hummed through the speakers, and there was a small stage for bands and karaoke.

I wiped a hand on my jeans. My fingers were pruning up from the condensation of my beer bottle.

What was I doing here right now?

It was like I had nowhere to be. My place felt wrong. This bar felt wrong. At some point, maybe I should contemplate if it was just *me* that felt wrong.

I was unsettled.

I couldn't unwind when there was no losing this tension that had burrowed its way into my chest the second my dad and I had dropped Lucy off at her house.

For some reason, I was trying to live my everyday life as if I hadn't dropped my heart off at Lucy's little cabin behind the Honeybrook Inn.

"Spencer. It's your turn."

"Huh?" I slowly focused on my oldest brother Hunter's face. We were in the pool room.

My brothers and I looked alike. Tall, with dark brown hair and light blue eyes, we looked like our parents had cut and pasted us into existence.

"Where'd you go, Spence?" His eyebrows popped up expectantly as he took a swig of his beer.

He knew what, or rather who, I was thinking about. Apparently, not talking about something did not make it a secret, which, by this time, I should have already figured out. They clearly had noticed I had a thing for Lucy over the years.

I considered opening up about her but decided against it. It was too soon. I should open up to *her* first without the pressure of trying to fight our attraction in the cabin to get in the way.

"Sorry, I'm just tired, I guess." I stepped up to the pool table and took my shot.

He didn't answer. His eyes flashed as he watched me, studying my face as I answered him.

"Knock that shit off, Hunter. Quit staring." I was antsy; my brain was filled with nothing but spiraling thoughts about Lucy, and all I wanted to do was get out of here.

"Yeah, leave the man alone," Deacon said as he wound his way toward us through the crowd, carrying fresh beers for us and a plate piled high with wings and fries.

He sat at the high-top table next to the pool table and dug in.

Tucker was home with his kids, who had begged for one more night with Larry. Brody was still working, so it was just the three of us. Dad had gone home after we dropped Lucy off. He was an early-to-bed, early-to-rise type of person and rarely joined us here unless it was a special occasion.

"Are you okay?" Hunter persisted.

"Yeah, of course. I'm fine." I twisted the cap off my beer and took a sip before setting it on the table next to Deacon.

"You were stuck up there—"

"With Lucy Darlington," Deacon added.

I glared at him, and he shrugged.

"Yeah, for what was it? Three days?" Hunter continued. "Why are you here with us right now and not with her?"

"Because I always come here? I don't know."

"But I think it's good you're here," Deacon said. "You have to make sure you still feel it."

"Feel what?"

"Whatever you felt when you dropped her off." He eyed me speculatively. "Dad said you were wrecked."

"I'm not wrecked. I don't want to rush her is all." I slid into a chair at the table. "I don't want to fuck this up."

"That's understandable, even smart," Hunter said. "Being stuck with someone is extreme. Maybe that's why you're so—" He waved a hand up and down. "Messed up."

"I'm fine. I swear." It was a lie. I was not fine, but they didn't need to know that.

Deacon sipped his beer as he watched me. It was obvious he was trying to figure out what I was not saying out loud. "Did you know Grandma and Grandpa only knew each other for five days before they got married?"

"Really?" My head whipped to his because I did

not know that. They were married for nearly fifty years, happy together until he died.

"Yeah, and they didn't even know each other before they got together, like you and Lucy do. Love at first sight is a real thing. I believe in it."

"I—why does this make me feel like I'm stupid for being here right now?"

"Because you have somewhere better to be." Hunter laughed.

"Is that Spencer Cassidy and his band of hottie brothers I see?"

Collectively, we spun around to see two of Lucy's half-sisters headed our way—the oldest two—Paige and Piper.

Paige's ex-husband owned this place, so I was surprised to see her here.

"Evening, ladies," Hunter drawled. Paige was his age; they'd gone all through school together.

"Hey, Hunter. Did you guys hear the news? I got this dump in the divorce. It's officially mine now."

She pulled up a chair and took a fry from the platter in the middle of the table.

"Congratulations?" Hunter chuckled. "Help yourself. Can I buy you a beer?"

"Nope. But this is on the house." She tapped our table as she scanned the crowd with ice in her eyes. "*My house,* she muttered before refocusing back on

Hunter. "Can I get *you* another beer? You three are the only ones here who are not shooting daggers at me with your eyeballs. It's appreciated." The pride in her eyes almost hid the hurt in her expression.

"We're fine. Thank you." He held his unopened bottle out to her. "You look like you could use this."

She took it, popped the top off, and then took a huge gulp before setting it on the table with a belea-guered sigh. "Thanks."

"Come on, Paige. It'll be okay—" Piper rested a hand on her shoulder before turning to me. "How are you doing, Spencer? We just left Lucy's place."

"I'm good—" My mouth hung open at least ten questions about Lucy butted up against themselves, trying to find their way out.

"Lucy is *good*, too." Piper leaned in conspiratori-ally, bumping my shoulder with hers before sitting next to me. "Something about the look on your face told me you'd want to know."

"He's got it bad," Hunter smirked. "Hasn't said a word about it, though."

Paige pushed the beer bottle across the table to him with a bold stare. He took it and finished it off, tipping its mouth toward her in a silent toast. "Thank you, ma'am."

"Well." Piper cleared her throat. "Lucy wasn't talking either. She had nothing much to say about what had to be an eventful few days. Isn't that weird?"

"Nothing at all?" I asked, my breath quickening at the mere thought of hearing any kind of news about her. "Uh, so what did she say?"

She met my eyes. "Just that you were a total gentleman."

"One of the few left in town," Paige answered me, but it seemed like she only had eyes for Hunter tonight because since she got here, they hadn't looked away from each other for more than a few seconds.

What the hell was I still doing here?

My hand drifted over my phone in my pocket as I contemplated texting her. Or maybe I should call her. What if I just drove over and stopped by?

"Do it," Paige told me with sharp eyes.

"What?" I huffed a startled laugh.

"Go for it. Take out that phone and use it, Spencer."

"You think I should?"

"Absolutely," Piper answered.

"Bye now." Paige wiggled her fingers.

"Yeah." I grabbed my coat off the back of the chair and slipped into it. "I think I'll take off."

"Don't do anything I wouldn't do," Deacon said.

"Nice, that means you can pretty much do anything." Hunter laughed.

"Hey—"

"Later," I called over my shoulder, already halfway to the exit.

Without another word, I strode the rest of the way to the door, flinging it open and rushing to my truck, practically jumping into it once the locks disengaged.

I yanked out my phone with my heart pounding a reckless beat in my chest.

Waiting was stupid when you knew your feelings were real.

I remembered her words from our first morning together in the cabin.

"I'm sick of dating apps and meetings in bars. I'm sick of playing games too. I'm also tired of seeing where things go while he's talking to five other women. If I see the letters WYD in a text one more goddamn time, I'll lose my mind. And I'll probably drop dead or end up in prison for murder if I get one more dick pick. I'm over it all."

It was time to start giving her what she wanted.

SPENCER: WYD

. . .

Shit. Maybe I shouldn't have sent that. God, I hoped she realized I was kidding. I threw the truck into gear and pulled out of my parking space.

I should just go to her. That text was an awful idea.

My text notification went off. Thankfully, I was at a stop sign.

LUCY: JAIL!! Immediate jail! No 200 dollars for you, evil, bad man.

I blew out a relieved sigh. Laughing out loud in my truck like a freak. Thank god. I texted her back, then took off again.

SPENCER: Is it too soon to say that I miss you?

Two notification *pings* in a row. I pulled over.

LUCY: I miss you too. So, no.

LUCY: Where's my dick pic? JK

SPENCER: Maybe you should see it
in person first. haha

LUCY: Good call. Maybe we should
meet for tacos later and see where it
goes.

SPENCER: I heard the weather is
supposed to be great tonight

LUCY: O.M.G.

SPENCER: Too soon?

LUCY: Never

SPENCER: What are you wearing?

LUCY: LOL I'm dying. I'm in my favorite pink nightie with a matching thong

SPENCER: Pics?

SPENCER: For the record. I'm JK about the pics.

LUCY: Maybe you should see it in person?

I pulled back onto the road. The Honeybrook wasn't far. I had to feel it all again. No waiting. I couldn't go home and call her. I had to see her. Now.

SPENCER: Look out your front window, sweetheart.

LUCY: RUNNING

Grinning, I opened my door and stepped out. Her place was cute. I could see her living here, writing her books, watching TV, being adorable, and living her life...

Fuck, I hoped I would be able to be part of it. I wanted to be with her here and at my place and everywhere, all the time. I needed her.

> LUCY: Wait. Confession: I am not
> wearing a pink nightie…

Laughing, I shoved my phone in my pocket. I didn't give the first fuck what she was wearing. All I cared about was having her in my arms again.

She came flying out her front door with her gorgeous butterscotch waves trailing behind her in the cold evening breeze just as I slammed the door to my truck to head up her driveway.

She did not stop, so I braced my legs apart and waited for her.

"Sweetheart."

I held out my arms and caught her as she jumped into them, wearing nothing but the hoodie she'd stolen from me and a pair of winter boots.

Upon further discovery, she hadn't been lying about the thong. She hooked her legs around my waist, ankles digging into the small of my back as I supported her with my hands behind her thighs, right below the bare skin of her luscious ass. I felt the edge of it with my fingertips, lacy and soft, and groaned out loud.

"You're here," she murmured into my ear, peppering my face and neck with sweet little kisses. "I couldn't fall asleep without you, so I wore your hoodie."

She smelled like heaven, like lavender and vanilla. Like forever and a day. Like she was mine.

"I should have never left you." I was breathless. It felt like I was home again with her in my arms. "If you tell me to come inside with you, Lucy, it begins. Me and you. We begin."

She pulled back to look at me. "Do you think it would be a mistake? That this is happening too fast?"

"Fuck no, I don't."

She sighed, arms and legs tightening around me as she buried her face in the side of my neck. "Good. I don't either. This feels so right. Come inside with me, Spencer."

I walked us up the path to her front door. "Where are we headed, the couch? Or…?"

We made it inside and I kicked the door shut behind myself.

"Take me to bed, Spencer. My room is straight ahead."

We didn't make it to the bedroom. I had to kiss her; I couldn't wait another second. Backing her up against the wall, I sealed my lips to hers, swallowing her sexy little moan and tangling my tongue with hers. Feeling for the first time all day that I had made the right decision.

I let her slide down the front of my body until her feet touched the floor.

She kicked off her boots and ran her hands up my chest. I shrugged out of my coat and let it drop to the floor behind myself.

"I am so happy you came over. You have no idea."

I brushed her soft hair over her shoulder, smiling down into her eyes. "I couldn't stay away anymore. I thought of nothing but you all day."

"Me too. I didn't want to wait for our date. I would have called you, but I didn't have your number. I also didn't have my car." She dropped her forehead against my chest. "I mean, I wanted to find you," she mumbled. "I was in full stalker mode, but I had no way to get to you."

"I'm so sorry." I cupped her cheeks and kissed the top of her head. "I'll never let this happen again. You'll always be able to reach me from now on. I swear."

"Okay. Is this too much? I can be a lot." Her voice shook and I wished she would look at me. "Should I back off?"

"No." With a fingertip beneath her chin, I tipped her face up. "No way. I've wanted you for so long, Lucy. I just wouldn't let myself feel it. Because somehow, I knew I had to be ready for you. That I had to be man enough to handle the way you have always, fucking *always*, made me feel. I shoved it down. I couldn't allow it until I could give you what you deserve."

"You're mine now, Spencer." Her eyes blazed as she gazed up at me. "Mine, okay? You're just gonna have to put up with all the ways I'm going to spoil you. I'm talking some seriously clingy stuff, so don't freak out, please."

"Yes to all of it." My entire face spread into a smile. "I want everything. There's no freaking me out, sweetheart. I swear. I want it all."

"Be sure, because I'm sure about you. I don't want to go back to the way we were. I don't want to lose this—"

"You won't lose me." I kissed her quickly before continuing. "Listen, I've dreamed of this. Of you and me. Together, just like this. I'm yours."

"I have too. So many times. You were in my dreams, Spencer, and now it's real."

"Yeah, baby, it's real. Who cares if it's fast? We know what we have. Nothing else matters."

"You're right. I want it. I want you, Spencer. Now."

Grabbing my hand, she tugged me down the hall and toward her bedroom.

It was pink, with a white four-poster bed, but strangely, I felt right at home in this girly cloud of a room, probably because I felt at home with her.

She slipped out of my hoodie and tossed it to me, leaving her in a lacy white thong that showed more than it hid.

"I have condoms—a huge box from Costco, uh, in my bedside table. I won't tell you that my mother drops them off every few months because she's overprotective in even the cringey ways. Yeah, so anyway, we have nothing to worry about." Her face blazed with embarrassment. She was fucking adorable.

"Promise me, Lucy. Swear you won't ever change or hold anything back. Ever." I bit back my laughter but couldn't hide my huge grin. "I think you know this already. But I'm falling for you, sweetheart."

"Thank god because I am too." She held her arms up, and I bent low to wrap myself around her, lifting her off her feet, kissing the side of her neck, and smelling the sweet lavender scent of her skin. I couldn't get close enough.

"God, you have no idea how many times I've imagined this." I breathed into her hair. "Your gorgeous body. Getting between these pretty thighs of yours. I've thought about how you'd taste way more than I should, Lucy. Now that it's real, I think I might lose my mind. You drive me crazy, and you've been doing it for years. I have never been more sure of anything in my entire life."

"This is happening. It's really happening."

"Yes, it is, sweetheart. There's no going back now. I want you too much."

"I want you too. The cabin was real, but it also felt like it was too good to be true, like magic or a daydream. You being here tonight means the world to me."

"To me too. I couldn't stay away from you any longer."

"You're wearing too many clothes," she murmured, wiggling to get down. "I want to feel you."

"Get on the bed." I watched her slip out of her thong and throw the covers back as I undressed.

"Oh. Wow, you're big." Her legs squeezed together as her eyebrows shot up. "I knew, in theory, I mean. Uh, that it was big because I felt it in the chair. But yeah."

"Don't worry. I will not hurt you. You'll be ready to take me, I'll make sure of that."

Her nod was slight. Her eyes had not yet moved back up to mine.

But my god, she was beautiful, from her pink toenails to her pink nipples to the pouty smile on her pretty pink lips. She was soft, with curves for days and those shining butterscotch waves flowing down her back.

But it was more than that. She wasn't just straight-out-of-a-dream stunning. She was in my heart. She lit me up. She had me feeling things I'd never felt before, and I never wanted this to end.

She sat on the edge of the bed, watching me with hot eyes and a sexy little smile as I prowled toward her, then tipped her back onto the bed to come down on top of her, giving her my weight for a second before straddling her, with my knees on the outside of her legs. I moved down her body, kissing a trail down the delicate column of her neck, between her breasts, and her softly rounded stomach before stopping to press a kiss at the juncture of her thighs.

"Can I? I want you ready for me. I need you so much."

"Ummm, I've never come like this. It might take too long. You don't have to."

"Have to?" I laughed, letting my forehead drop to her stomach. "Poor Lucy. You should only ever be with a man who begs to go down on you." I tipped my head up, resting my chin on her belly button.

"God, Spencer." She breathed. "Are you serious right now?"

I darted up to kiss her lips. Then pulled back, smiling into her pretty brown eyes, watching her face change from hesitant to hot. She wanted it but was scared to take what she wanted.

"I'm dying to taste you." I groaned against her

mouth. "Don't you know that? Remember the top four?"

She nodded.

"It's number one now. You have to come first. You need to be ready for me before we go any further. Should I beg? Would you like that? I'm already on my knees for you and I'm not afraid to say please."

Her eyes got big. She didn't answer.

I kissed and licked my way up and down her body, taking one pink little nipple into my mouth, sucking hard, then releasing it with a pop.

"Please, sweetheart." I nipped at her earlobe. "Trust me, I'm going to love everything about this, and I don't care how long it takes to get you to come. I could spend the entire night right there between your pretty legs and be perfectly satisfied even if this is all we do."

Her legs dropped open one then the other. I slid down her body and licked from her opening to her clit. Smiling against her slick, soft skin as she went boneless beneath me.

Gripping her hips, I licked into her, causing her to squeal, but I held her hips and teased her until she was writhing against my face, rocking against me, needy, desperate, and already close to losing herself.

"I'm—it's happening. Oh god, Spencer."

"Let go, Lucy. I got you."

"I—can't."

"Do you need to say please, sweetheart?" I pulled away and darted my tongue against her clit. "Tell me to make you come, Lucy, and I'll do it. Ask me for anything, and I'll give it to you. Beg me for it, and it's yours."

"I—please, Spencer. Oh god, please, please, please..." Her eyelids fluttered, the swoop of her dark lashes making shadows over her cheekbones as she sunk her teeth into her bottom lip.

I sucked her sweet little clit into my mouth and drove a finger inside her, hooking it up to find that spot that would make her fly apart.

She was stunning.

She was everything beautiful in the world.

She was mine, and I was hers, and this was never, ever going to end.

I watched her; she was so close, almost there, biting her lip, grinding against my mouth, and trying to keep her moans inside. Fuck that, I wanted to make her scream, so I sucked harder, flicking my tongue and adding a second finger. I smiled against her slick skin when she squeezed it tight.

The muscles of her neck tensed, and her feet dug into my shoulders. She raised her arms above her head, gripping the headboard tight in her fists as she came for me. From the inside out, her body undulated beneath my hands and mouth in a beautiful, rippling wave as she cried out my name.

"Now you're ready for me."

I fumbled in her nightstand drawer for a condom, sheathed myself, then sank inside of her. I groaned out loud at the feel of finally being enveloped in her tight, wet heat.

"Spencer," she moaned in my ear. "You were right. You feel so good inside of me."

"God, you're like heaven. You're it for me, Lucy. So perfect."

Her scent was in my beard—honey and spice mixed with the sweet smell of lavender as I buried my face in the crook of her neck and fucked into her. Slowly at first, then I picked up my pace as she dug her fingernails into my back and wrapped her legs around my waist.

"Please don't stop. Oh god, Spencer. Please."

I shifted my position, then took her hands in mine, pressing them into the mattress as I thrust into her, faster, harder, until we fell over the edge together.

Chapter 21
Lucy

Like I weighed nothing, he moved me so I was settled against him, head on his chest with his arm around my upper back, fingers running through the ends of my hair as we came down, panting together, and I wondered if we were still on earth.

Moonlight shone through the slats in my window blinds, casting him in shadows and flickering light as he lightly stroked a hand down my arm.

He was so beautiful that it almost hurt to look at him, but I did anyway, tipping my face up to find him gazing down at me wearing an expression I'd never seen before.

My heart seized as I grew warm and content. Spencer made me feel safe, beautiful, and special, and I loved it.

"Are you okay?" he whispered, his voice filled with concern.

"Please know that I am. I'm perfect. I've never felt like this before," I answered, tracing meandering patterns across the broad wall of his chest with my fingertip. I was not yet sure if I should be mortified or proud of myself for letting go enough to come so hard. "I mean, I screamed "yes" so freaking loud. And your name, maybe God's name, too. I can't remember." I lifted up on an elbow so I could see his face. "Was I too loud?" I squinted in the dark, watching for his reaction. "Tell me if I was, and I'll try to rein it in next time. But I don't know if I can, considering how you make me feel."

Amused eyes met mine. "No, you were not too loud, sweetheart. That's what I was going for—you screaming my name. I'd consider it a failure if you didn't."

"Oh. My god. You get more amazing with every word that comes out of your mouth." I settled back against him again, pressing my cheek to his pec. "Well, I'm happy to oblige. You're welcome to do all of that to me anytime. I am a fan of your work."

"I plan on doing all that to you every day into eternity if you'll let me."

He brushed kisses over my cheek, tangling his hands into my hair as he held me close.

I threw my arm over his chest and my leg over his waist like one of those stuffed Velcro monkey things and held on. "You're never getting rid of me, Spencer."

"Good." He squeezed me tight, taking my hand in his and kissing the back of it before pressing it back to his chest. "Because I'm never letting you go. Never again."

"Stay with me tonight?"

He turned to his side, so we faced each other. "Yes. I would love that. I don't think I can sleep without you anymore, Lucy."

"Isn't it amazing that this feels so easy?" His eyes crinkled at the corners as he grinned at me. "I almost don't trust it. Being away from you today was terrible. Everything else has been like a dream come true."

"If our biggest problem is we can't get enough of each other, then I think we'll be okay." He leaned forward and kissed me softly.

"I think so too," I murmured against his lips.

"Goodnight, sweetheart." He kissed me again, darting his tongue into my mouth and pulling me closer.

"Sweet dreams, Spencer."

He smiled at me as his eyes drifted closed, letting out a soft sigh as his body relaxed and he fell asleep.

I watched him for a few minutes, wondering how I got so lucky. Spencer looked like the walking, talking definition of toxic alpha masculinity, but inside, he was a marshmallow. Even when he made me beg, he was sweet.

I drifted off to sleep, wrapped in his arms and dreaming of a future where I could look into his beautiful blue eyes when I woke up in the morning and every morning after for the rest of forever.

Chapter 22
Spencer

Friday Night Date

There was something I hadn't said to her yet. Tonight would be the night I told her I loved her. I didn't care that my feelings and intentions wouldn't make sense to a lot of people when you considered the timeline of our relationship. She was all I cared about.

Lucy had blown my world open and filled it with everything I didn't know I needed, and now I couldn't live without her. I didn't want to try.

There was no such thing as *too fast* when you were in love. Love was the only thing that mattered. I knew that now.

Time didn't matter.

Perception didn't matter.

She was the only thing that mattered.

Lucy was rapidly becoming my best friend. She was funny, smart, clever, and completely weird. I adored every crazy thing that came out of her mouth.

We had spent every night together, at her or my place, and only separated when necessary for work. Our kids got along—my dog and her fish. They loved staring at each other through the glass of her aquarium.

We were in sync. Nothing was ever a discussion or a fight because we communicated our needs effortlessly. We naturally took turns cooking, cleaning up, and taking care of each other.

I knew it was because we were ready. We found what we had each been seeking and were beyond happy to have it. We'd fallen into a seamless rhythm as if we'd been together forever.

Tonight, I would tell her everything. How I felt about her, how much I needed her in my life, and that I was in love with her. She probably already knew, but words were almost as important as actions, and I hadn't said them out loud yet.

She was at her house getting ready for the date I'd asked her out on before we left the cabin. And I was at the cabin doing the same. I was also here getting everything ready for our date.

I'd cleaned the place from top to bottom, decorating it with candles and flowers from the Misty

Meadow Flower Shop in town. Then, I ordered Lucy's favorites from The Honeybrook Inn's restaurant—I had asked her grandmother what to get since we hadn't eaten there together yet.

This night had to be perfect, and I'd done everything I could think of to make it so, including replacing the box of condoms in the bathroom.

I bent to stuff the paper bag into the cupboard, frowning when I saw that a bag with a note written on it was already in there.

Spencer,
Maybe I messed things up for you by not replacing these sooner.
But I will never ask, and you will never tell.
I'm sorry. Or not. I don't know, and I don't want to know.
We will never speak of this.
This never happened.
-Deacon

I dumped it on the counter.

Condoms.

I huffed a laugh, then put the boxes in the back, wadded up the bag, and tossed it in the trash.

After one last look in the mirror, I grabbed my keys and headed to my truck to pick Lucy up.

It was cold, but the skies were clear as I drove to her place.

I wouldn't mind getting stuck up there with her again, though. My life made more sense when it was just the two of us.

As I pulled up, I saw her peeking through the curtains. When she spotted me, she closed them with a swish, and I smiled in anticipation.

Walking toward her felt like stepping into my future.

I knocked, waiting for her to open the door.

Her shoes clicked on the wooden floor, and I held my breath.

"Spencer." She breathed.

She was dressed to the nines, in a dress with heels, a full face of makeup, and deep red lips. She was so stunning that I didn't know where to look first, so I let my gaze wander over her as I took her in.

I closed my eyes, overcome. "You're so beautiful." I breathed.

Her laughter floated up from her throat. She knew exactly what she was doing to me, and it was sexy as fuck. "You're not even looking, silly. Open your eyes."

"I can't. I'll stare, then we'll stand here all night. Me struck dumb, and you looking like a fucking goddess."

"I'll never get over the things you say."

I opened my eyes. The dress was midnight black, with long sleeves and a deep V-neck. She was taller in her black spiked heels—the better to kiss her—and looked beyond gorgeous. A blush from my words decorated her high cheekbones, and her cherry lips smiled at me.

"You're stunning tonight. This dress is amazing."

She grabbed my tie, pulling my face to hers. "Thanks. I bought it so you could take it off me later. It zips all the way up the back. Isn't that fun?"

"Yeah, sweetheart." *Fun.* She was a fucking dream come true is what she was.

"You look gorgeous, Spencer. That suit suits you. You're dapper and handsome, and I don't know what I like better, your fixing cars, blue-collar hot guy clothes, or this."

"You don't have to choose." The air between us was electrified. We'd be lucky if we didn't jump each other before we got to the cabin. "You can have all of me."

"It's like I won the lottery or something." She reached inside the doorway then handed me her coat. I held it open while she turned and slipped into it. "Where are you taking me?"

"It's a surprise." I held her arm as we walked to the truck. The driveway was slippery from the rain.

Her hands on my arm tightened. "I bet I can guess!"

"I bet you can't," I shot back. Getting her riled up always led to good things.

"I'll start guessing once you start driving."

"That's too easy." I opened the passenger door to help her in. "This is a small town. We don't exactly have a lot of options up here."

"Fine." Satisfaction pursed her mouth as she tilted her head, and her eyes flashed with humor. "The cabin."

"Ah." I waited a beat, trying not to give it away. "Do you want me to tell you if you won?"

"No." She wrapped her arms around my neck and pressed a kiss to my throat. "Wherever you take me, I'll win. As long as I'm with you, I can't lose."

"You're the best thing to ever happen to me, Lucy."

I looked into her eyes, and the whole world faded away.

But once I got on the road, I didn't look at her at all. I wanted her too much. Luckily, the drive to the cabin was quick.

Chapter 23
Lucy

The gravel crunched beneath the truck's tires as he turned onto the private road leading to the cabin. "I knew it! I won."

"What happened to wherever you take me I win?" He chuckled, slowing down as we approached the cabin.

"I can have both things, right? Why choose?"

"You can have anything you want, baby." He glanced over at me. Every time his eyes met mine, my heart turned over in my chest.

"That's what I like to hear," I teased, knowing it worked both ways. I would do anything for him too. Always.

He pulled to a stop and cut the engine.

"How about, I love you. Do you like hearing that?"

"What?" I spun toward him, hair flying over my

shoulder. "Say it again. I want to see it too. Wait, let me —" I unbuckled and climbed into his lap. "Okay, now tell me. I want this to be multisensory."

"God, I fucking love you."

"I love you too."

He seized my cheeks in his big palms and kissed me. His hands drifted into my hair, and his tongue swept into my mouth. Straddling him on my knees, I felt him hard underneath me, so I sank down with nothing but my panties and his dress slacks between us.

He pulled back. "Holy shit. Let's get inside, sweetheart. Before we end up having to make a mad naked dash into the cabin."

"Yeah." I panted. "That was—something." I opened his door and carefully climbed down. "I like how "I love you" sounds when you say it."

"I love you," he repeated, eyes blazing down at me.

"Gah! I love you too!"

He joined me on the ground, swept me into his arms like a groom with a bride, and carried me to the porch.

"Those shoes are sexy as hell but not made for up here, baby. You'll slip and fall."

I threw my arms around his neck and kissed his cheek. "They're doing what they're made for, Spencer. Aren't they?"

"I guess they are." His eyes crinkled at the corners as he grinned at me.

After setting me down, he unlocked the door and swept out an arm. I went inside, taking a few steps into the living area before twirling in a circle to take it all in.

"What did you do? It's like magic in here."

A fire blazed in the fireplace. Candles in cute little jars were placed throughout the room, and gorgeous arrangements of pink roses were centered on the kitchen table, the fireplace mantel, and the end tables.

"It is magic whenever *you're* here. You've changed my life, Lucy. Since the minute I saw you way back in kindergarten, it's been you. You've always been special to me. Then you drew that picture of my mom for me, and I told my dad I would marry you someday. I don't remember saying it, but he reminded me the day he picked us up. But this cabin is where we truly started, and I thought it would be the perfect place to tell you how fucking in love with you I am."

"I love you, Spencer." I threw myself into his arms. "More than anything. I'm so lucky I crashed into that stupid snowbank. I never thought it was possible to be this happy. But somewhere in the back of my mind, I always knew it would be like this with you. You're the magic, Spencer. You've changed my life too."

"I love you so much."

"And I love you. I'm going to make you happy. I promise."

"You already do, sweetheart."

We broke apart, staring into each other's eyes and smiling like lovestruck fools as we realized how good we would be together and how lucky we were to have found something this special.

Chapter 24
Spencer

"**I** got dinner from the Honeybrook," I told her as she slipped out of her coat. "All of your favorites. I asked your grandma what to get."

"See? You're the magic."

I took her coat, slipped out of mine, and hung both of them on the hook by the door, watching her as she wandered further into the room, smelling the flowers and looking at the candles while admiring what I had done.

She stopped when she got to the chair—*our* chair. I watched her intently, aching for her touch, knowing that everything we felt for each other would explode out of control tonight.

"I want you now." She said and our eyes locked. "I want to get in this chair with you and finish what we started the other night."

"Like I said." I crossed the room to stand in front of her. I towered over her, but somehow, she was the one in control. "You can have anything you want."

"I want you to take off your clothes and sit down."

I tossed my suit jacket on the couch and got to work on my tie. "You got it."

She turned around, "But first. Unzip me."

I slid the zipper down, baring the lovely alabaster skin of her back and groaning out loud as she let the dress fall to the floor.

"Keep the shoes on," I ground out.

A soft smile unfurled across her face as she looked at me over her shoulder. "You can have anything you want too."

"I know, sweetheart. But all I want is you, and anything you're willing to give me will always be enough."

With her hands on my chest and a wicked smile on her face, she pushed me back toward the chair.

I kicked off my shoes, shed the rest of my clothes, and then sat, breathlessly watching as she bit her lip and glanced at me as if contemplating where she wanted to begin.

"I like how you're looking down at me right now. Waiting to find out what you're going to do does it for me. I fucking love it."

"Don't stop talking. I love the things you say."

"I liked it the other night, watching your face as you ground yourself against me. You were so hot, so fucking wet for me I could feel it through my clothes. But it will be so much better this time."

I reached for her, sliding my hand between her legs and pushing her panties aside to circle her clit. "You're already wet, and I've barely touched you. You need me, sweetheart, don't you?"

"Yes."

"Say it."

"I need you. I want you. God, Spencer. I love you so much."

"I love you too. Get those panties off, sweetheart."

Hooking her fingers in the sides, she shimmied out of them and straddled my lap as I slid a condom on.

"We need to take this chair to your place," she whispered, hovering over me. My dick twitched in anticipation. "I will never be able to handle seeing anyone else sitting in it."

I chuckled. "Straight to my bedroom."

"We'll hide it in the closet, just for me and you to use whenever we want."

"Nobody else allowed," I growled into her skin and nibbled on her neck. "Hidden, where all you are is *mine.*"

"I'm yours. I'll always be yours, Spencer."

Leaning back in the chair, I watched her, groaning

as she stretched wide to take me inside, hearing her sweet little gasps as she moved up and down, leaving me slick with her desire.

It was like ripples on a pond, then waves crashing over rocks. Harder and faster until we were moaning into each other's mouths as we kissed, desperate to fall over the edge together.

With a shudder, she collapsed against my chest as I lost myself in her.

"You're my favorite place to be, Lucy. You're my home."

Chapter 25
Lucy

One Year Later

Spencer was on one knee.

I was dressed in my warmest winter attire.

Fireworks were shooting off above us. Real ones, not metaphorical, even though I was so thankful for him and the fireworks he made me see every day.

The Honeybrook Hollow New Year's Eve Firework show was in full effect. The town center was still decorated for Christmas and Skipper McFadden was hosting the festivities.

Spencer was proposing to me as fat snowflakes plopped on our heads, and my mind was whirling.

It was supposed to be a clear night—we all should have known better.

"I promise to always love you. And I swear on my life that I'll never leave you. Because without you, my heart won't beat. I need you to live, Lucy. You're everything to me. Will you marry me?"

"Yes."

He slid a round, brilliant solitaire on my finger. Then, he kissed my hand as I sank to my knees on the blanket we'd been lying on to watch the fireworks and kissed him all over as we fell to the ground, wrapped up in each other and the magic we'd made together.

About the Author

Nora Everly is a lifelong bookworm. She started reading the good stuff once she grew tall enough to sneak the romance novels off the top of her mother's bookshelf and it has been non-stop ever since. Once upon a time she was a substitute teacher and an educational assistant. Now she's a writer and stay at home mom to two small humans and one fat cat. Nora lives in the Pacific Northwest with her family and her overactive imagination.

Find her at noraeverly.com
Get all the Nora News!

Also by Nora Everly

The Sweetbriar Mountain Series:

In My Heart

Heart Words

From the Heart

Heart to Heart

Change of Heart

Cross Your Heart

Sweetbriar Holiday Stories:

Holiday Hearts

Conversation Hearts

Honeybrook Hollow:

Next to You

Make You Mine

By Your Side

Meant for You

The Cozy Creek Collection:

Fall at Once

Oh Brother!

Crime and Periodicals

Carpentry and Cocktails

Hotshot and Hospitality

Architecture and Artistry

Teachers' Lounge

Passing Notes

Star Crossed Lovers:

(*As Piper Everly, co-written with Piper Sheldon*):

<u>Midnight Clear</u>

Get exclusive sneak peeks of upcoming releases through Nora's newsletter and Facebook group, The Everly Afters.

www.ingramcontent.com/pod-product-compliance
Lightning Source LLC
Chambersburg PA
CBHW010800310726
48974CB00006B/920